Erratics

To Patti –
My friend and fellow
short story writer.
Best Wishes
Roger Hart

Erratics

Roger Hart

—Winner, George Garrett Fiction Prize, 2000—

Texas Review Press
Huntsville, Texas

FIRST EDITION, 2001

Requests for permission to reproduce material from this work should
be sent to:

Permissions
Texas Review Press
English Department
Sam Houston State University
Huntsville, TX 77341-2146

Stories in this collection appeared in the following journals: *Am-
bergris*, *The Ohio Writer*, *Other Voices*, *Passages North*, *Potato
Eye*, *Rosebud*, *The Sun*, *Willow Springs*, and *Foliage, a Short
Story Quarterly.*

The author wishes to thank the Ohio Arts Council for their
support and the Poetry League of Cleveland for featuring "My
Stuff" in their literary showcase at the Cleveland Playhouse.
He especially thanks Dave and Diane for kindness and a
place to write and John Gerlach, mentor and friend.

Cover design by Paul Ruffin
Cover photograph by Roger Hart

Library of Congress Cataloging-in-Publication Data

Hart, Roger, 1948 May 30-
   Erratics / Roger Hart.-- 1st ed.
      p.   cm.
   ISBN 1-881515-37-0 (alk. paper)
   I. Title

PS3608.A787 E77 2001
813'.6--dc21

                              2001040657

To Gwen,
for more than words

Table of Contents

1   My Stuff

12   The Fence

25   The Woman in the Front Seat

33   Below the Surface

48   Erratics

60   Lines

75   Lubing: Sex and Symbolism

            Beneath an '88 Buick

84   Chautauqua

95   Charades

104   Numbers

111   Fire

122   Cecil's Highway

erratic: *a rock or boulder displaced from its original location by glacial transportation. Common in Ohio and the Midwest*

Les

My Stuff

Time was I could fix anything with my fist or foot. *Bamm*, the furnace started. *Bamm*, the refrigerator quit humming. Cindy didn't like it, but there wasn't much she could say when it worked. Take the time the lawnmower died in the tall, gummy grass where the neighbor's dog unloaded in our yard. A Saturday morning. Hot and humid with bugs flying in my ears and biting my back where the sweaty tee-shirt stuck, and this rank odor coming up from all that dog crap. The mower coughed, choked, then stopped. Blue smoke and steam came from underneath. I pulled the starter rope. Nothing. I yanked again and again until I thought my damn arm would fall off, then grabbed the mower by the handle and spun around like a hammer thrower in the Olympics. I grunted, let go. A flying lawnmower. It hit the trunk of the silver maple. Moldy grass, rusty lawnmower parts and maple bark littered the ground. I swore at the son of a bitch, then let it lie there, bleed lubricants, while I went in the house, had a beer, maybe two.

Cindy said, "Look what you've done to the tree, look at that tree," then said that it was too early to drink, and I said I was on daylight savings time, which was pretty clever considering the heat, bug bites, and the mower not working. I waited awhile, watched cartoons with Jake, then went outside and tried again, pulled the rope. Flames six inches long shot out the exhaust. The engine roared like the Saturn V taking off for the moon. I could have mowed down the lilacs, roses and rhododendrons if I'd wanted.

Cindy didn't like my swearing either, but I said, "Hey, a man's got to talk."

Ohio summers can be bad but winters are worse. Snow, cloudy days, fog, the lack of light, the cold wet wind blowing off Lake Erie.

Muscles tense from slipping on ice, people get moody, think bad thoughts.

I drive for the county, a snowplow in the winter, an asphalt truck in the summer. Winter of '76, our worst winter ever, I knocked off thirty-two mailboxes. A record. That winter Cindy hit me but it wasn't because of what I did to the mailboxes, although she didn't like that either. I was tired from plowing all night and when I opened the refrigerator door things fell out. It was like food and bottles and bowls attacking me. I put my foot inside and began to stir things around, kick this and kick that, fight back. More things fell out: A-1 Sauce, milk, orange juice, leftover lasagna. Cindy came out of nowhere, knocked me away, almost knocked me off my feet. She was crying and yelling at me to stop and the chocolate syrup was running out onto the floor, and my foot wouldn't, couldn't, stop kicking.

Later, we cleaned up the mess and fixed the broken refrigerator shelf and wiped the tomato juice off the stove where it splattered, but the red stains on the wall and the way the shelf tilted always reminded us.

Cindy taught fifth grade, made greeting cards, sold them at craft shows. After our problems, after I had moved into this apartment, she sent me a card that had a buckeye leaf—Ohio, the Buckeye State—on the front of it. Inside, the card said, "Be-leaf in yourself."

Three hundred bucks a month and the bedroom has a tiny jail-size window, but it doesn't matter because I don't have a bed. I sleep on the couch in the living room, listen to television and people sounds from the apartment below. The phone in the kitchen doesn't work because of problems with wires in the wall, and, when I moved in, the silverware drawer was littered with marijuana seeds. O.K., his real name is Oscar Kurt but he goes by O.K., said the seeds were from the previous tenant, a man he had not liked. O.K. is the manager of the apartments. O.K. and his wife. He said he was sorry for not cleaning out the seeds when he painted the apartment and that I should toss them out. "No," he said, "better burn them or flush them down the toilet so they don't sprout somewhere and cause a problem." O.K. gets a tumor in his head but that hasn't happened yet in this story.

Alone in the apartment. A boring life except for planting those marijuana seeds and sometimes watching the woman in 214 undress behind her thin curtains. With binoculars, I can see tan lines almost.

Jake! What a boy. When he was four we went ice skating. He was a natural. Glide, cut, glide. A speed skater, another Eric Heiden. He'd skate towards me and I'd spread my legs, and he'd skate through. Swoosh! We were like the United States hockey team beating the Russians. Following year, we went skating and he was even better, but he had grown and when he tried to skate between my legs, his head smashed me in the balls and I nearly died out there on the ice, another broken winter thing.

Jake doesn't talk to me much since this last bad winter when Cindy and I had our differences. I try calling him, but my phone sometimes doesn't work, and if Cindy answers, she goes on and on about "my problems." I dial anyway, punch the wall, wait, swear, then walk to the gas station on the corner and stand in the phone booth, stand on broken glass and sticky spilled pop, breathe in the stink of cigarette butts and hear the cars, trucks and vans going down the street. A crummy place to talk to your kid. I press the phone tight to my ear and yell things at the passing cars and trucks, give them the finger while I listen to the phone ring.

"Yes," she says, Jake's mom, like she knew it was me that was going to call. "Yes? Yes?" like she'd already said it a dozen times and this was the last.

"Jake, please," I say.

"Your stuff," Cindy says.

"My stuff?" I ask.

"Your stuff," she says, and then, "You going to Jake's soccer game?"

I say, "Yes, of course, and what about my stuff, and can I speak to Jake?" I shift my weight. Glass crunches.

"You said that last game," she says, and then she says a *friend* will be at the game with her and that Jake can not come to the phone.

"Where's Jake?" I ask.

"It's *Les*, *Les* from the fire department. You know him, Les Huddle."

"Les?" I ask. I want to talk with Jake but this Les talk has me confused.

She says, "Yes, Les," and that I shouldn't forget my stuff, that it will be in the trunk of her car, and before I can ask for Jake one more time, she hangs up.

"Les?" I say. "Les?" I say it to the cars going down the street. I feel as if I've been smacked and scraped by a snowplow. Cindy seeing a Les. I get a pain in the middle of my forehead, like I was stung there by a wasp. I'm a Les, too.

I head back to the apartment and am followed by a dumped-off dog. Brown, curly hair down its back. Big paws, sharp, white pup teeth. "Go home," I say. "Go home." She sniffs my shoe. "Go," I repeat. "Go on. GIT!" I slam my foot on the ground. She stares, brown eyes rimmed with red, a hungover dog.

I give her a bath in my tub and then a bowl of stale cereal that she scarfs down. The apartment's hot, real hot because it's on the second floor, which is cheaper, and because it's August, but the dog shivers like she's about to freeze, so I take her outside in the sun. She does her chores on the grass, then sits on the toe of my boot. Back inside, I throw a ripped jacket on the floor, and she starts a nap.

O.K. comes, knocks on the door, says he saw me with a dog, and he saw it making a pile out there on the lawn where the little kids play, and we can't have that, can we?

I say I'll clean it up and point at her sleeping on the jacket, the spot in the sun, tell him how the dog is gone as soon as she finishes her nap. I jerk my thumb at the door. "Out of here," I say.

O.K. says, sure, sure, waves his hand in the air like he's shooing mosquitoes, slurs his words, says he has a headache, then shakes his head like a hound with a bug in its ear. Sure.

August. The marijuana plants are ten inches high, and Cindy's seeing another Les.

Jake thinks I don't like soccer because I ask the wrong questions, say the wrong things like, "kick a goal," when that isn't his thing to do, and I have missed the first three games. Cindy says he's angry because I left him. She jabs that word, *left*, like a knife in my gut. *Left*, RIP! *Left*, SLASH! Cindy says that Jake's full of anger and will have to work it out. "He's a good kid," she says. "You left him, but he's a good kid."

I get a kick out of soccer: balls bouncing off heads, referees waving yellow cards in front of faces—those who've sworn or tried to hurt somebody. "There, take that," the referee says, holds the yellow card above the player's head so everyone can see who the guilty one is. Jake hasn't gotten any yellow cards, although he's been warned.

I got the big red card from Cindy. Out of the game! A red card. The worst. Not a divorce really, a dissolution, although Cindy called it a "dis-illusion."

Doris sleeps beside the couch in a cardboard TV box I got out of the dumpster. I got the couch for nothing, found it in the middle of the Shoreway while plowing. Dropped by someone moving, someone trying to escape Ohio winters. One cushion has tire marks, but the couch is comfortable so I don't bother buying a bed.

Doris—I named her after Cindy's mother—rides in the truck with me to the game. It's raining hard and the turning this way and that makes Doris sick. Real sick. Soggy cereal all over the floor. She gets a guilty look after she tosses but I don't say anything. I've been there. I think fresh air, roll the window down and push her head out, hold it there until we get to the school. When we stop, I throw the floor mat out in the parking lot; Doris licks from a puddle to wash that bad taste out of her mouth, then climbs back in the truck to get some sleep.

I squish through the grass toward the sidelines. Soggy socks, wet feet, Jake on the field, pretending not to look for me. Cindy and her new Les with a clot of friends in the bleachers, chummy beneath their umbrellas. Cindy motions me over and says, "Les, this is Les."

We say, "Hi, Les," at the same time. It sounds funny in the wet. Cordial. I can feel the others taking time out to watch so they can see how the mechanics of these things work. I say I think we'll win this one, start to tell them about Doris, but they turn away, don't answer. I'm not part of the clot, but I sit close enough to be part of the cheering when good things happen and to hear kind things said about Jake.

Cindy hangs onto Les Two, holds his hand, rubs his back, his neck, punches his arm, puts her head on his shoulder. If Doris could see it, she'd get sick again. I sit and wonder if Cindy ever says, "Les," thinking me, but it being Les him. He wouldn't know, but she would. Maybe that's why she hangs onto him so, trying to make up for thinking the wrong Les.

I start to climb higher for a better view and slip on the damn bleacher steps. Aluminum. Whoops! Just like that. I go down three, four, maybe more steps. Boom, boom, boom. Hurt my damn hip and I want to say the f-word twenty times which I'm trying to give up on account of the way Jake has picked it up and is using at the wrong times.

People in the clot say, "Ooh, are you okay?" and "Be careful there." Then they give each other the secret look because they think it's the beer. No one invites me to sit with them, hide under their umbrella. My pants, wet and cold, cling to my leg.

I no sooner stop my moaning than the other team bounces the ball off a head and into the net.

Back and forth, up and down the field, knees pumping, elbows flying. Jake gets knocked down, his feet tripped from under him. "Hey, hey," I yell. Jake jumps up kicks the ball, runs, slides, kicks again. "Way to go, Wright!" I yell. I say "Wright" so he hears it, his last name, remembers how good it sounds. "Way to go, Jake," Cindy yells, a shriek that almost stops the game.

My hip throbs, and I worry that I've broken something but I watch the game anyway. Jake's team is running down the field like looters in LA when the referee blows the whistle, throws his arms up and gives the ball to Fairport. Once, twice, three times it happens. No one says what for, and I can't stand the not knowing so I turn to the umbrellas and ask, "What's going on?"

My hip bone hurts like hell, and I'm nearly drowning in the rain, but I need to know.

"Jake's offsides," someone throws out. I don't know offsides. I'd know if it were football, but soccer players run everywhere, no huddle, no *hut*, *hut*. I nod at the umbrellas and pretend I understand.

People say Jake and I walk alike. We roll along, our legs swinging back and forth like wet noodles, our asses not doing anything fancy except bringing up the rear. I figure Jake and I'll stop at McDonald's after the game, grab some hamburgers and fries, maybe a couple vanilla shakes, too. We'll wet noodle walk in together, and people will nod and smile. We'll scatter packs of sugar on the table, move them this way and that, and he'll explain offsides. Jake and me, his dad.

Fairport scores four more, Jake's team none. Game over, rain coming down. Jake and the others drift across the field, wet and muddy but no one in a hurry.

"Nice game," I say.

Jake gives me the dirty look, the one he's learned from his mother.

"Let's get something to eat," I say.

"Too tired," he says.

We walk toward the parking lot, me on one side, Cindy and the new Les on the other. She puts her hand on Jake's back, which isn't a good thing to do as that is one of the first things that'll get you called candy-ass, and Jake has enough of a burden with those offsides.

"A milkshake?" I ask.

"I'm tired," Jake answers, staring at the ground, at his feet going slop, slop, in the puddles.

"Next time," I say.

"What?" says Jake.

Cindy throws her hands in the air. "Your stuff," she says. "I have a box of your stuff in the trunk."

But this is no time for stuff talking. I slap Jake on the back. "Next time we'll get something to eat."

"Oh," Jake says, and he climbs into the other Les's car. The trunk lid is up, waiting, and Cindy is standing there with her hands on her hips, but I need to get Doris home, so I wave good-bye and head out.

When I get to the apartments, an ambulance is backed up to O.K.'s, the red flasher lights bouncing off wet windshields, the brick walls and everyone's windows. Curtains are pulled back, and flat-nosed faces stare out. A dozen or so people stand in the parking lot and watch, hold themselves tight.

The radio hums, and the medical people talk back and forth, but I don't know what's happening. It's like the offsides. They slide a stretcher inside the ambulance, and O.K.'s wife tries to climb in too. "O.K.," some guy says and two women give him a dirty look. Doris and I stand with the group on the corner. Feels good to be part of a knot, but feels bad for O.K., who is not. My hip hurts like hell, but it isn't the time to tell anyone, hope for a little sympathy. No one knows what's wrong but we stand and talk, me and a guy from another building and a young woman from the apartment below mine who runs every morning. Tom. Rita. Rita lets Doris lick her face.

Next day, Rita knocks on my door. "What's your story," Rita

asks. Rita looks nineteen, wears snug jeans and scratches Doris's belly with red fingernails.

I tell her I nearly broke my damn hip and the phone doesn't work when the apartment is hot, and she says that O.K. has a brain tumor, a big sucker. She hands me a card to sign and asks if I want to chip in for some flowers. She bends over and pets Doris again; the blouse gapes open. Skimpy, black bra. I give twenty bucks, wish I could give more.

The brain tumor scares me. Cindy used to yell that I must have a brain tumor the way I acted. A week passes, two. Can't get it out of my mind, his tumor, maybe mine. Gives me a headache. I think maybe I've got something ugly growing inside, that living here in the apartment has caused it. Cindy used to say that the drinking would kill my liver, but here's a tumor popping up in O.K.'s head for no reason.

So. I'm sipping beer and thinking and I dial Cindy to say I've waited long enough and I want my stuff. The phone won't work, and I start yelling and swearing and beating on the wall. Doris runs to the corner by the stove and shakes. I say, come here, but she can't for all the shaking. I punch the wall and I think she's going to drop dead of a heart attack.

I try dialing again and Les answers and I forget what I'm going to say. "Hello? Hello?" he goes and then the forgotten thought comes to me and I say, "May I speak to Cindy?"

Les Two tells Cindy it's me for her, then whispers that I've been drinking, like he doesn't think I can hear and like he could tell over the phone, which shows what a jerk he is.

Cindy says, "Yes," and I say the manager of the apartments is back, and she asks where he's been, and I tell her about the brain tumor and that it had nothing to do with drinking. She asks if I am alone and can she talk freely. I say, yes, except for Doris.

Cindy waits for me to say who Doris is. I wish I'd named Doris *Cindy*, just so Cindy could know what it's like for me. Her seeing another Les. But I don't tell her who Doris is and she—Cindy, not Doris—says it's too bad about the brain tumor, and she's tired of carrying my stuff around in the back or her car, and if I don't get it soon she is going to pitch it out.

I say, "I have to see Jake, we need time together." Doris trembles in the corner. "Come here," I say, but Doris sticks to the corner like she's nailed there. Cindy says no way she is coming to my place.

I tell her I want to speak to Jake, and she says not to push him, that he's tired and angry and I need to give him space. "Come here," I repeat. I move toward Doris and she squats, pees a puddle on the floor.

"No!" Cindy answers.

I say she doesn't sound too upset about O.K.'s tumor and tell her Doris is trembling, shaking like a buckeye leaf in the corner, and Cindy asks if I'm drinking but doesn't give me time to answer. The line goes dead. Maybe Cindy, maybe the heat.

I could punch the wall again. I could yank the phone out. I want to and I would except Doris has this shaking problem and is going to flood the apartment downstairs if she doesn't get control of herself. I stand there wondering what's wrong with Doris. I get a handful of Sugar Pops off the table, drop some on the floor. She doesn't move.

I toss a Sugar Pop in her direction which lands in the puddle and Doris ignores it, just stands hunched over in that wet spot. I toss another Sugar Pop across the floor, another. One bounces off her head and she doesn't even notice. I cross the kitchen, almost pull the damn phone cord out of the wall because it's wrapped around my arm and I forgot to hang up. Doris trembles. First O.K., now Doris. I hold her tight, stick her nose in my armpit and after a few minutes the shaking stops.

Because the phone's not working I don't get many calls: "Hey, Les, come on over. The game's on, and there's plenty of beer," or, "Dad, want to go see the Browns?" So I walk Doris mornings and nights along the railroad tracks that run behind the apartment. I figure if she tires herself out she won't chew on the electric cords or steal garbage from the wastebasket and will get over the nervous condition I suspect she has.

I walk the rails and think how the tracks go nowhere, not to Dallas, not to Santa Fe. No place like that. No place different from this.

Doris has instincts. She'll sneak up on bottles and beer cans, freeze, lift a paw. Her point isn't the best, being young and mostly retriever, but somewhere in her blood she knows: one paw up, tail out, body stiff, nose sniffing the air. She holds her head high, looks up in the night sky like she's seeing birds except her eyes are on the moon and stars. An astronomer dog almost. While we walk, I talk, tell her things. "Doris, the moon," I say and I tilt her head in my hands until I think she sees it.

Sometimes I let Doris pull the leash while I lean back and study the sky, find the constellations. Long time back, Cindy was surprised I knew them, Ursa Major, Cygnus, Cassiopeia, the Horse Head Nebula, there in Orion, in the belt. Amazing stuff. "How do you know them?" she'd ask, like I might not be smart enough. I taught her ten constellations and the names of certain stars. On summer nights, we'd lie in the drive, look at them through a telescope I had, a telescope still wrapped in garbage bags in the basement of the house where I used to live.

After the next under-the-lights night soccer game, I tell Jake, "I have someone I want you to meet." As we walk to the parking lot you can see the wheels turning in his head, him thinking it's some woman, which tells you something about the stories his mother has put in his head. Cindy looks angry, Les Two smug. I open the tailgate, and Doris jumps out.

"That's Doris?" Cindy asks.

"Doris," I say, "meet Jake."

For a second, Jake grins, although they lost the game. "You need a leash," he says.

"You can't keep her in the apartment, can you?" Cindy says. "I mean, I don't see how you can keep her in the apartment."

Instead of saying she's a cute dog or something like how Jake will have fun with her when he comes to visit, she starts off talking about the problems. She glances at the other Les like he might help her with this, like he might chime in and say, "Can't keep a dog in the apartment."

But he stands there not knowing what to say.

Her seeing another Les is not a good thing—not that Lesses are bad apples or anything like that. But, if he, Les Two, did something stupid and Cindy said to the teachers at school or to the women she walks with, "Les lost his job," or "Les lost three hundred dollars playing poker," or "Les was drunk again last night," I don't want people confusing which Les it was. And Jake. What if he hears someone say, "That Les, what an asshole"?

By the time O.K. comes home from the hospital the leaves are off the trees, it's snowed twice, Jimmy C. has lost the White House job to Ronnie "Wagon Train" Reagan, Jake's team has lost ten games, Doris can find Venus almost, and Cindy has heard talk, wants to know if I am living with that young girl.

Rita offered to take care of Doris when I was plowing snow, and I said that would be fine, but she is not the other woman Cindy thinks she is although it would be okay with me if she was. I barely know Rita other than catching the glimpse of her lace bra and some of what was in it.

It's good to talk to a dog, tell them stories. They pick up more than you think. I tell Doris things. I tell her about Jake skating between my legs, and how soccer season is over. No more games, I say.

We walk along the tracks and there are things I want to tell her that I don't know the words for. "Look, look," I say, pointing to the sky. "Millions of stars. Millions. I sit on the rails, pull Doris to my side. Doris puts her cheek, smooth and soft, against mine, her breath warm, our eyes on the night sky. Orion, Lyra, The Big Dipper. I show her Polaris, the North star, and explain that it's the one to use if she's ever lost.

The cold from the rail I'm sitting on creeps through my pants, my butt goes tingly then numb, and I tell Doris it's time for us to move on. Six in the morning, stumbling down the tracks, me and Doris, chunky gravel loose underfoot, cold December kicking off Lake Erie. The moon huge at the end of the rails.

Doris. What a dog. I could say, *fetch moon*, and she'd try. She'd bounce on those hind legs and snap at the cold night air until she passed out. I could tell Doris to fetch the moon but I don't. Doris is young and doesn't understand distance.

The Fence

Fifteen feet high. Heavy wire mesh. Three rolls of concertina tangled through it. Barbs like knives, razor-sharp, poking out of rolls of wire that never rust. Ordinary barbed wire I could have climbed over and out. I'd have been punctured, but I could have done it. Concertina? It would have sliced me up, my blood running out until only clothes and bones were left hanging on the fence. Besides, the guards in those towers watch, wait, play with the triggers on those twelve-gauge shotguns. Couldn't scratch without them seeing.

The fence. It was so bad I thought I'd die, my heart freeze up. I was like a muskrat caught in a trap, ready to chew off my leg to get out. The click of the steel door was like someone pushing my head under water, holding it there.

Nothing ever got out. Not much got in. Some bugs, a bird. The wind floating up through the trees carrying smells and sounds from the town of Nelsonville.

My first month it rained a solid week. I could smell the rain at night from my bunk. I had rain dreams, this water pouring down on me so hard I couldn't see or talk. I wondered where it was all coming from and a few here who have found religion said the Lord was trying to wash this ugly place off the Earth. Someone else said the rain was the leftovers of a hurricane that hit Florida and slid north, poured itself out on Ohio.

Good thing this place for troublemakers, perverts and bad apples is on a hill.

When we finally got outside, there was this tightness in my throat. I tried not to look at the rolls of wire, the steel mesh. I took deep breaths of the sweet free air coming up the hill, gulped it down and held it in my lungs, my chest sticking out. I thought if I got enough free breeze inside it would help. Beyond the fence, birds chirped, tires screeched, a train shifted to a siding, a car horn honked.

Behind me, Norm, my bunkmate, was doing laps, sixteen to a mile. Every four laps he'd change direction, do a few push ups. Some days he went sixty laps, more. Macho man.

Norm slapping his feet around the track. Two guys from Toledo tossing rubber horseshoes against a rubber pole: thud, thud and non-stop bitching and moaning whether one was a leaner or not. I faced the fence, breathed deep, tried to store that air up in case another hurricane came, and we didn't get out the next day.

Somewhere beyond the fence there was the WHOP! of a fastball hitting a catcher's mitt. Made me smile. Strike one, I thought. I stepped closer to the fence, stared off into the trees on the other side. I smelled hot dogs and mustard, heard boys chatter, "Hey batter, batter," and pretty soon the whole game came floating up to me like big-screen TV, like I was sitting behind first base. One second I was staring at trees, the next, I was watching baseball. Nelsonville versus Lancaster. A pitcher's battle. I caught every sound, the crack of a foul ball off the bat, the umpire yelling, "STEeeRIKE!" I could see the puffs of dust when the first baseman kicked the bag, the center fielder brushing the hair from his eyes, the pitcher dropping the rosin bag behind the mound. I could see it all, every inning, even with my eyes closed, this game coming up through the trees. Score tied in the bottom of the ninth when one of the Nelsonville locals whacked a pitch over the left field wall. Nelsonville 2, Lancaster 1.

Game ended and I was back staring at the trees on the other side of the fence. I looked around. No one else had seen it. I knew I'd tapped into something big.

No cells here. Dorms. Like a college with bars and armed guards with nervous twitches sitting in towers, dreaming of you running so they can shoot your ass. The whole depressing place surrounded by that fucking fence. The light at the end of the floor stayed on all night, a bare bulb, a beacon for anyone heeding nature's call. If I turned my head, took a quick glance around the room, it would have been like waking up from an operation and knowing something was missing, a hand, a foot, your heart. Had to open the eyes slow, look at the ceiling cracks an arm's length above my head, give the mind time.

Crazy Norm in the bunk below never slept. Eyes always open,

shooting eye-bullets through the mattress, into my back.

He would have been in maximum security for all the bad he'd done, except he was sixty-three and some fool figuring a sixty-three-year-old Norm too soft in the head for serious fights. Five times arrested for assault. (Once with a pipe, which he said he just happened to find.) Five! I got eighteen months for growing some pot beneath a few grow lights in my apartment, weed from seeds that were left in a kitchen drawer. Only made a few bucks and Bamm! the door got kicked in and I was being cuffed like I was a drug lord. Still, Norm had the bug up his bung that I got off easy and he had ten more to complete his twenty.

He wasn't big, Norm wasn't. Not small either. Built good for a man his age, but it wasn't his size or muscles that scared us. It was those polished black stone eyes, animal eyes caught in headlights, Charles Manson eyes. Bolt of lightning temper. Bad attitude. An anti-social son of a bitch. All in his glare and stare. He once slapped George, the glass company embezzler from Toledo, bloodied his nose, all for George pointing a finger at him. "Don't point your finger at me," Norm said. Whack! Knocked Greedy George down, blood squirting from his nose like oil from an Oklahoma well.

Norm had everyone thinking he sneaked into town at night. Even some of the guards. Morons! Thinking he could get through that fence. Norm, a head case and a fake.

Breakfast: the smell of grease and eggs from the kitchen came to us mixed with the stink of garbage and disinfectant, stale air and the one hundred twenty sweaty bodies in that wing. There was the weight of the fence and the blue uniforms, green walls and the entire day stretching out like some deep, dead ocean.

Norm sat across from me, an empty chair on each side of him. Sit next to him and he'd push those pointy elbows of his into your arm until you had no room at all. Hurt like hell. Complain and he'd slap you out of your chair. A certified liar and a sneak. My bunk partner. Couldn't read shit but pretended he could. Carried letters around in his pocket for weeks at a time. A sixty-three year old con holding a one-page letter in front of his face for half an hour tells you something.

Marvin and Lloyd sat at the end of our table. Both from Lancaster. I hated that town. Perverts, degenerates. Lloyd, who ate his mother-in-law twenty-seven years ago, spent twenty locked up at the max in Lorain before being moved to Hocking with the understanding that he was old and not the cannibal he once was.

Swiss steak every Sunday, tough and stringy, had to cut it with the pop can tabs we sharpened on the bricks and carried concealed and illegal in our pockets. Every time I tried cutting the meat or was grinding those tendons between my teeth someone whispered, "Hey, maybe Lloyd would like that." Some argued about what mother-in-law parts he could and could not have eaten, others said it shouldn't be a crime. All this, while the tendon was stuck in my throat.

Lloyd could be forgiven for munching on the mother-in-law, but Marvin I can barely talk about. Marvin, a drug dealer from Lancaster who was an assistant—sit down for this—*prosecutor*. A law man. No secrets here. Marvin—you name your kid Marvin, you've got to expect problems—showed up with his head shaved, but still looked like the law, so I figured he was going to have a hard time, which was okay by me. Marvin prosecuted Baxter over in C wing and got him five to ten without parole. I knew Baxter had a score to settle and he would get the law man, even things up a bit.

But what happened? Marv—I swear that's what they called him, Marv—got legal questions and respect like he was a one-man supreme court.

"Can I appeal?" "Can they send me back?" "Can I file bankruptcy from here?" "My old lady sent me this," and they'd shove an official looking envelope in his face.

Ex-lawman Marvin would pull on his chin, smack his fat lips, tap the envelope and say, "This will take some time and it'll cost."

Lloyd and Marvin at the end of our table. I couldn't look. Marvin and Lloyd and General Sherman, who burned up the South, all from Lancaster, Ohio, twenty miles up the road, these Hocking Hills being a dangerous, shameful part of this Buckeye State.

I sat, sipped my coffee. After a minute, we'd get in line, get toast, cereal, maybe rubber eggs. Some spit on their food before they ran for more milk or another cup of coffee. If they didn't, someone would take the good stuff like fruit cocktail. Norm could have left his seat for a week, left a cup of fruit cocktail or chocolate cake—if we had any—and no one would have ever messed with it.

Norm rocked back on the hind legs of his chair, almost fell over, recovered, glared and rocked back again. He touched the pocket of his shirt, the letter.

I said to Norm, "My ex married another Les." I figured it was something no one had ever heard of before, a woman leaving one Les to marry another, but he didn't smile, he didn't nod. I told him that in my whole life I only knew of two Lesters other than myself and she, my ex, married one of them. I would have told him about my son and how he is a soccer star, but I didn't like bringing Jake's name into this place. Norm looked away, maybe bored or deaf, his stomach moaning like a whale in heat.

Lloyd, the meat-eating pervert, came along, raised his hand like he was going to pat Norm on the shoulder, stopped. "Saw your shoes this morning, Norm," he whispered. "There beside your bunk before roll call. You tracked in some grass during the night. How you do it, sneaking out like that? You sure are something, Norm."

Norm bit his toast, chewed.

"You sure are something, Norm." "Grass on your shoes, Norm." "How you do it, Norm?" "How you sneak out of here, Norm?" Made me want to puke, which wouldn't have been hard to do.

Norm shot Lloyd with the crazy eyes, and Lloyd shuffled away, shaking his head and muttering, "Sure is something."

Metal trays clanged on the tables, chairs scraped on the floor, pots and pans banged in the kitchen. Fourteen more months. I had an ache deep in my chest, thought I'd die.

The Indian guard, Native-American-Tony, came over, looked around, up and down the table. "Norm," he said.

Norm didn't answer.

"I know," Tony said.

Norm played with the spoon, moved it back and forth on the table.

"Next week I'm on nights. Hear?" The black Indian eyes waited.

Norm spun the spoon.

"Not next week," Tony said. "Not while I'm on duty." He shot me a look like I was Custer, then walked away.

Others stopped, shook their heads. "Town? Is it nice?" "Women? You see any women?"

Norm wouldn't say squat.

"The women pretty, huh? You meeting someone?"

Norm dunked burnt toast in that sticky egg yolk, swallowed, sipped his coffee, swallowed. He turned the evil eye on them, spit menace and toast crumbs across the table. They backed off. Norm picked up his tray, carried it to the kitchen.

I followed him back to the dorms. Three buildings with bars on the windows and rows and rows of bunks. You could walk around in your dorm as much as you wanted as long as you caused no problems and avoided those who thought you might want to steal from their footlocker. Stand by your bunk at six, noon, six and ten for roll call. Wear your ID badge at all times, the picture of you with the shaved head, frowning, looking scared or mean.

Norm went to his bunk, swept up the grass clippings, clippings he probably put in his pocket the day before. He swept them up, making it look as if he didn't want anyone to notice. He'd been doing that off and on since I'd joined him in this pervert zoo.

I heard that some mornings in the winter Norm had snow melting off his shoes. He was a fake though. A fake with a mean streak, the worse kind.

He knew I knew. Not that I ever said anything. Everyone else said, how's town? Can I go with you? Why do you come back? All that shit, but I just sat and listened, smiled my smile, did my chores, cleaned the windows, watched the clouds, waited until we could go outside.

Each day I hurried to the fence, to the spot between the horseshoe pits and the softball field, a spot made special by the tree shade on hot afternoons and a cool breeze that came up through the woods, up from the town of Nelsonville below, the spot where I saw the baseball game. I stood close to the fence, felt the weight of it, and I waited for something new to come through but nothing did.

I heard stories about those who had taken off, but no one I knew ever tried, except Norm, and he didn't count because his sneaking out was faked. The old ones, the ones who had spent their entire lives inside looking out, and would probably have dropped dead if they ran, sometimes mowed the grass, pulled the weeds on the other side. Two took the warden's car into town. That's one story. Tried to fill the car up with gas but had no money. Drove around for awhile, sat in a park down by a river, then came back. No place else to go.

It wasn't electrified, the fence. I thought maybe it was at first and that was how the signal, the picture of the ballgame, came to me like television. If a softball or horseshoe hit it, an alarm went off. Hronk, hronk, hronk. Like a nuclear submarine. Dive! Dive! Guards running. Roll call. Line up immediately. IMMEDIATELY! Show them your ID badge, your name and number, the picture of you with the shaved head. They'd put a check beside your name, there on the clipboard, send you back inside, bad kids returning from recess.

So I stood and waited. Nothing. I went back everyday, stood there on the special spot, waiting for it to happen again. A week passed. Two. A month. Sometimes, I thought the game had been a hallucination, the long-term effects of too much beer or pot messing up my brain cells. Still, I waited, hoping the magic of whatever it was would happen again, and while I waited, the tightness in my chest came back and I couldn't sleep at night. I almost couldn't breathe.

One day I was by the fence thinking about the woman who had lived below my apartment and how her blouse would gape open, giving me peeks. I felt as if I might never see another woman again and I almost flung myself at the fence out of desperation when a car door slammed. The whoosh and bang of metal. It didn't mean anything, but I held onto it, played it again in my mind, the sound bouncing off the trees. It began to take on a shape and color, the cheap metal sound of a small car, domestic, faded gray, a '78 Mustang, worn tires and bad muffler, antenna bent back. All that from the sound. Craziest thing, like I was plugged into cable or a satellite.

A woman coming home with groceries. Alone. Jeans, faded, soft and snug. No belt. A bright red blouse. White tennis shoes with a little hole in each toe. Tiny ankles, small wrists, a mole on her neck.

And there was this old house, front porch sloped like the deck of a sinking ship, paint flaking around the windows, shutters missing slats. She stood on the buckled sidewalk, looking around as if she knew someone was watching, then she clutched the grocery bag, which was slipping out of her arm, and climbed up the steps, skipping every other one. She kicked open the door and went inside, the screen slamming behind her.

She dropped the bag on the kitchen table and started putting things away: buns, pop, hot dogs to do on the grill, some beans. Behind me all hell could have been breaking loose, Norm slapping someone silly, a knife fight, Marvin trying to bean one of the batters in the softball game, but I was there with this woman.

She put the groceries away except for one of the buns, which she took out and started to eat, just the plain bun and a can of diet pop. Then she got out a road map and unfolded it on the table,

pressed it flat, brushed away the bread crumbs and traced a highway across its surface.

I leaned forward. Her nails weren't painted, not chewed on
either. No rings. Part of my mind was watching and part was thinking how I wanted to say something. Pretty day. Where are you
going? That's some sandwich you've got there.

You know.

I stood there moving my lips, thinking about her hands. It didn't
worry me, watching all this. I didn't think I was going crazy or
anything.

She finished the bun and sipped her can of pop and all the time
she was looking at the map. Then she rummaged through a kitchen
drawer next to the silverware and found a few thumb tacks, pinned
the map on the wall, stepped back. The entire kitchen covered with
maps.

Maps to everywhere.

Then I got slapped on the back and the sirens were going
HRONK! HRONK! HRONK! and they were yelling at us to line
up, fall in. The woman disappeared and I saw trees and fence. I
turned, saw Norm glaring at Marvin and Marvin throwing back a
smirk.

A buckeye fell out of a tree and landed at my feet and the guards
were yelling, "FALL IN, FALL IN!" The buckeye was shiny, red-
dish brown, almost black, the color of the woman's hair. I bent over
like I was fixing my shoelace and slipped the buckeye inside my
sock. Usually, when they see you pick something up, some guard
comes over the bullhorn, says drop it, but this time no one said
anything.

For several days I couldn't go back outside to my spot by the
fence because of more rain, but I thought about her and the maps
and her hands and the way she swung the screen door open with her
foot. I'd think about her all afternoon and when I stood in line and
when Norm was sitting across from me at supper with a blue envelope sticking out of his pocket. Thinking about her made breathing
easier.

A week later, when I got back to the fence, to the special spot,
I had to stand in a puddle of water, but I stood there, water seeping
into my black state shoes while I tried to tune in to what might be
going on on the other side. Five minutes passed. Nothing. Ten,
fifteen. I held the buckeye in my hand, rubbed it with my thumb. I

stood there, my feet getting wet, waiting.

"What the hell you staring at!" blasted four inches from my ear, and it scared me so much I nearly jumped over the fence. Marvin, the drug dealing ex-prosecutor from you know where. "You in love with that fence?" He stared at me, the stale smell of breakfast on his breath. "Well?"

I didn't say anything. There was a car horn, and I held up my hand the way Uncle Bill used to do when we were hunting bucks in Pennsylvania and he'd hear a dry leaf crunch or a twig snap.

We stood there. Marvin, staring at me, waiting for an answer. I turned back to the fence but all I could see was the wire. I couldn't even see the trees on the other side.

I went back to the spot by the fence whenever we were allowed outside. Leaves changed. Leaves fell. I stood and stared through the fence at the maples, oaks, shagbark hickory, some scrubby sassafras, the buckeye tree. I'd think about her and those maps. My thoughts went wild, thinking if it was Christmas and I was on the other side, I'd get her a new pair of tennis shoes or a sweater, a red one, because she looked so good in red. I'd think about the three of us—Jake, my son, would be there too—sitting around eating cookies and looking at those wall maps, playing games of where we might want to go. Sometimes I'd plan ahead, think: today I'm going to hear her singing or raking leaves, the metal tines scraping the walk. I'd think it out, how it might happen, but every time I got to the fence Marvin was standing there smiling. I'd worry about him making a smart remark or slapping me on the back or throwing the softball against the fence, and I couldn't focus on anything beyond the wires.

I stood there, the buckeye in my pocket, trying to remember what I did, where I was looking, how I emptied everything out of my mind. I looked at the trees in the direction of where I imagined her house to be and worried that she'd left, taken one of those maps off the wall and a can of diet pop and headed for places friendly and far away from the angry Hocking Hills.

Nothing.

By November, it was cold and the clouds were swollen with tons of snow. Most of the leaves were off the trees and I could see further into the woods on the other side of the fence, but I still couldn't see any sign of the town at the bottom of the hill. No houses, no cars, no stray dogs or cats. Behind me, Norm did laps on the cinder track. Crunch, crunch, crunch. A demon man going nowhere.

One day, I heard a small engine start. A leaf blower or log splitter, maybe a mower making one last pass over the grass. I was concentrating when Marvin walked between me and the fence, snorted, smacked his fat lips, said, "Boo," in his snide ex-lawman voice, then headed for the track.

Crunchcrunchcrunch. He walked even faster than Norm.

"Hey!" Marvin said, "I hear everyone thinks you sneak out of here at night." Marvin put his hands on his hips, planted himself in Norm's path.

Norm went around him, kept on walking.

"Bullshit," Marvin said.

The horseshoes stopped thudding against the rubber pole. Ten thousand blackbirds squawked out of the trees.

"Bullshit," Marvin said again. The guards in the towers held their breath, maybe flipped the safeties off their guns.

Norm crunched around the track, didn't even give him the evil eye.

It's what everyone talked about at supper. I could tell by the way they pretended they weren't looking at Norm. I wanted to ask them where their heads had been. Did they think he had a key to the front gate or something? Morons and fools.

But it did burn me some, Norm's trickery being pointed out by Marvin, the former prosecutor from Lancaster, the town of degenerates and arsonists. Besides, he was my bunkmate.

After supper, Norm sat on his bunk staring at a one-page letter. Marvin was across the way, two packs of cigarettes on his footlocker, discussing legal matters with a wife beater.

"At least Nelsonville beat them," I said to Norm.

Norm looked up like I wasn't making any sense whatsoever, and I remembered that he didn't know about the game, the one that came through the fence. I hesitated, then moved down so I was sitting next to him which was a risky thing to do. He looked at me in his crazy way, and I could tell he was thinking about knocking me off, but I said real quick that there was a game between Nelsonville and Lancaster. He looked at Marvin when I said, "Lancaster," Norm's eyes sparking with those lightning bolts. I told him how the big toothy grins on the Lancastrians got wiped off when the local slapped a high, outside pitch over the left field wall. I told him how it all came to me through the fence.

Norm studied Marvin, whose grown-out hair was slicked back, oiled and shiny.

Then, Norm stared at me, the eyes dark and dangerous.

"There's a woman," I said.

He smiled, but not much.

"She lives at the foot of the hill, beyond the trees." I described the maps on her kitchen wall, the holes in her tennis shoes, and how I wondered if she'd moved away.

Norm sat and waited.

"Nothing happens anymore," I said.

Norm tilted his head back, gave me a look that said, get to the point.

"Maybe you could check," I said, "go by the next time . . . you know, see what you can see. You do that?"

Norm stared at the green wall beyond our bunks, maybe imagining those places where rumor said he'd gone. He didn't blink.

"I'd owe you," I said.

Norm fingered the letter in his hand.

I nodded.

We sat there.

"Could you take her something? Could you do that, leave it on her front porch?" I asked.

Norm gave a small nod.

Later, after all the lights were out except for the bare bulb at the end of the hall, I gave him the buckeye, my initials scratched on one side. LH.

Put it on her porch? Someplace she'll find it?

Norm took it without answering. An hour later, I heard his bunk springs groan, watched him go down the hall. I didn't believe he could get out, not really. I figured Norm was hiding behind some door or standing in the shadows waiting for a few hours to pass, before he sneaked back to his bunk. But he was my bunk partner, and after Marvin made fun of him in front of everyone, made fun of his supposedly sneaking out, I had to do something.

I couldn't sleep. There was snoring, coughing, whispers here and there, bed springs creaking. I listened for the siren or a guard yelling.

Four o'clock. Five. I was wondering what the hell he was doing, what was taking him so long, when there was a loud thud from across the floor, the sound of knuckles hitting bone. Someone moaned and a few seconds later Norm's bunk springs squeaked. He was breathing hard.

I waited. Lights came on, guards came in. Made me nervous as hell and I didn't know why. The guards passed the bunks one by one, checking names off a clipboard. Adams, Adamowicz, Brewer, Carlyle. They went down the floor until they got to Marvin. Marvin sat up, blood running from his nose, dripping over his blanket, his lip split and swollen three times its usual fat size.

Tony the Guard looked at his nose and lip, then looked across the floor at Norm.

Norm shrugged.

For a whole minute no one moved. It was like when a movie stops.

Tony gave Norm a small nod no one else was supposed to see, then he turned back to Marvin. "Better be careful, looks like you toss around pretty hard in your sleep."

The guards smirked and left and everyone started breathing and talking.

I looked down at Norm for signs he'd been outside. I knew he hadn't, wasn't possible, I was just looking, but when I didn't see any grass or dew or dead leaves on his shoes, I got that trapped muskrat feeling. I looked at Norm and he looked back, his animal eyes glaring like I'd done something wrong.

I didn't ask if he'd found her place or if he'd left the buckeye or if he'd seen her old Mustang with the bent antenna. I couldn't pretend I believed him that much.

Breakfast, wash the windows, mop the floors, lunch.

Afternoon, I went to the fence, to my spot. Any day it was going to turn real cold. I listened to the breeze and the birds, sniffed the air, the smell of dead leaves.

Norm walked over, gave me the dirty look again.

"What? What?" I asked. I saw Marvin standing over by the softball field, hands in his pockets, his swollen lip sticking out so that it looked like he was pouting.

Norm touched his head, glanced at the fence.

I started to say, no, nothing had happened, but at the last second changed my mind. "She's there," I said, nodding up and down several times to convince him.

But Norm stared at me, waited for more.

"There's a small white candle in the kitchen window. A small white candle and the buckeye beside it. How about that? I can see it," I lied, "the buckeye and the candle, the flame flickering in the breeze."

Norm stood there, the envelope sticking out of his pocket.

I started to tell him thanks, offer to read his letter, but before I did, the odor of vanilla-scented wax came up the hill, through the trees and the fence.

I stopped, took a deep breath, held it in my lungs, waited.

The Woman in the Front Seat

Blond hair, not too long, not too short. Blond, the color of ripe wheat with a few streaks of gold here and there. Fine hair. Soft. At least it looks soft. In the sunlight I have squinted looking at that hair.

Small nose.

The lips smile, smirk, grin, grimace, mock, quiver. Not big lips. Large enough.

And eyes. How wide they open! They look this way and that. Alert and telepathic.

I can't see the dimple below her eye or the color of her lipstick, except when the lights of an oncoming car almost blind me. She sits in the front seat, sits sideways and talks. I sit in the backseat and listen.

Not really. I don't hear a word. I see her lips move, see her eyelashes curling up, curling down, blinking.

I'd lean forward and touch my finger to her face, her forehead, maybe let it run down the tip of her nose, over the curve of her lips. I'd trace the entire outline of her face if I could. Forehead, nose, lips, chin, neck. But I can't. He's driving and she's his wife. He might look around and go off the road or into another car. He might punch me or swear or ask what I was doing. He might wreck, and even if he didn't, it would be awkward.

Very.

Let's say he doesn't notice my finger tracing the outline of her face. The woman in the back seat is my date. For sure, she'd see. She's not prone to violence and doesn't swear much, but she might make an exception if she saw my finger tracing the other woman's face, especially the lips, and how could she miss if I did?

I don't know what the woman in the front seat would do. With everyone watching I'm pretty sure she'd have no choice but to pull away, act embarrassed, ask what the hell I thought I was doing.

The man in the front seat and the woman in the back talk about the Cleveland Indians. They talk trades and who is needed and who is not, then they say they are hungry, say they want to stop and pick up some ice cream, maybe bananas and pop and fudge and potato chips, something salty, something sweet. They talk about the sundaes and splits they're going to build, things three scoops high. The driver says we read too much, the woman in the front seat and me. Got to do things, he says, can't be too cautious, life's too short, he says. He turns on the radio, pokes the buttons but can't find the game or the song he wants although I catch part of a good one before he clicks it off.

Songs. Last week I had an empty spot and stopped at the ice cream place. I sat in the car, in the parking lot, licking the cone, listening to the radio, watching little birds hop across the pavement. I heard this song which you've probably heard, a beat that goes to the foot bones and crawls up your legs, rhythm so nice and slow you want to sway back and forth and clench your eyes tight shut, but you don't because someone might be watching. That song. If she'd been there, I'd have asked her to dance. Right there in the parking lot, the two of us and that slow song, rocking back and forth among those hungry little birds.

I wouldn't have done it. Not really. I'm all talk and sometimes I'm not even that. Guilt. I feel guilty thinking about dancing with her. I'd have been guilty to death if I'd done it. And I know guilt.

Still.

The man in the front seat keeps talking about food, about ice cream, and I think of those little birds and that song and dancing in the parking lot. Maybe, no one would have noticed, faces buried in their own cones.

Recently, I was at a party, a wedding reception at a friend's house overlooking Lake Erie. I find a corner at parties, sip ginger ale and watch, talk to one person at a time. Mostly I like to listen, and, because I can't hear out of one ear (left), I want to see your mouth. See the words. At a party, eyes go around the room like searchlights at an airport. You see people you know, maybe you nod or raise an eyebrow, but they're over there with a drink in one hand and a couple cashew nuts in the other, and it's too noisy to shout through twenty people so you lift an eyebrow or your drink or your cashew nuts, and the person you see does the same and the eyes keep moving.

When the searchlights aren't going around the room, they stare at the mountain painting on the wall or the Zuni fetishes displayed on an end table or try to sneak a peak at some woman's legs. But at this party our searchlight beams, hers and mine, locked on to each other like a malfunction. One, two, three, four seconds. No nods or lifted eyebrows, just the locked beams, then they'd start up again, going around the room or back to the stone coyote there beside the dish of nuts. It happened two, three times.

And this: she touches my arm when we talk, the forearm part which is skinny and not muscled at all, but she'll touch it and say I don't know what because I'm thinking about her hand on my arm.

I might not notice these things, the fingers on the forearm, the broken searchlights, except for what happened when I was living at a state-run facility in the Hocking Hills part of Ohio. Let me explain. I might have died there, my heart just dried up and stopped if it hadn't been for a vision—that's what Tony, the Native American guard, called it when I told him about it a few days before the end of my stay. "A vision," he said.

I was standing by the fence and I saw, I visioned, a woman. I mean, there were trees and trees and trees on the other side of the fence and you couldn't see anything else. Just those trees. But one day while I was standing at the fence staring out, trying to get some air in my lungs, I heard a car door slam and then I saw a woman. It was like I was at the movies or watching a big screen TV.

She was carrying groceries into her house and I could see her shoes, the tiny holes in the toes and the scar in her ear where an earring might have been and a mole on her neck. Everyday, all I wanted to do was get out to that spot by the fence and see her. I imagined buying her Christmas presents and the two of us painting the old house she lived in. Her kitchen was covered with maps, and I'd spend nights and rainy days trying to imagine where she might be going, hoping she wouldn't leave until I was out, and then maybe I could go with her too. I'd dream about the two of us in her car driving somewhere at night, following a line on one of those maps, her face lit up by the dashboard lights.

When your time is up, the state of Ohio gives you a bus ticket back home and some guard drives you to the bus station there in Nelsonville. I wanted to walk around town, try to find her, but there was no way that I could. Day after I got home, I drove back to Nelsonville, a scary thing to do. I walked up and down the streets for an entire day, but I never saw her or that house.

Two years passed. Nothing. Then, last year I was at Jake's soccer game—he was a senior—and the woman sitting in front of me turned around to ask why the referee kept blowing the whistle. I almost fell out of the bleachers. It was her, the woman on the other side of the fence. I stared and stared and almost hugged her on the spot, but I controlled myself.

I didn't tell her where I'd been or how I'd seen her on the other side of the fence. I didn't ask if she already knew. I said I was Jake's dad and that she looked familiar. "You too," she said.

I missed some of the game for all our talking and then when I was screwing up the courage to say something personal, say something about how I'd seen her before and maybe we could go out for a milkshake or something later she said, "Oh, here comes my husband."

A cop was walking towards us, and at first I had the feeling he was coming for me. But he was coming to sit with her. The man and woman in the front seat. An amazing thing, but there is another: we all became friends.

Eventually, there were other things I noticed, like when I got my tooth pulled last month, for example.

We were in the car, the four of us, coming from someplace, and I was getting a wisdom tooth pulled the next day. It was my fifth, which there is a name for, and everyone started telling tooth-pulling stories of blood and pain and cracking noises, which I knew on account of my experience with the other four, and she turned around as I was getting out of the car and squeezed my arm and said, don't worry, and I said, thanks, and her fingers hung on, didn't let go as fast as you'd think married fingers would. The squeeze meant something, the pressure of her fingers, although I still spent the evening worrying about the pain and blood and cracking noises.

The man in the front seat says he sure is hungry, and he leans forward over the steering wheel like that might help him find food. But I'm not thinking food thoughts—I'm thinking about the woman's face, her voice, a voice that is husky and deep, a night voice, a voice that surprises me when it comes out of her thin, feminine body but delights me, too.

I sit with my arms across my chest, my hands squeezed under

my biceps, try to focus my thoughts elsewhere: I think of how the Browns were stolen from Cleveland and that not enough people appreciate the beauty of Lake Erie. I think of the dog I once had and how I'd like to get another. It doesn't work. She blinks and I can hear the eyelashes slap together almost.

No one would believe it if I were caught dancing with her, running a finger tip down her face. They'd be flabbergasted. He did WHAT? they'd say. Then they'd go on and on about how hard it was to believe. They'd shake their heads, but give them time and someone would say, "You know, I wondered about—" and they'd say our names. They'd pull on their chins and shake their heads and say our names again and someone might say how I had spent some time you-know-where and that I never could be trusted. Or they'd mention how we were always talking about places we wanted to go and taking those imaginary trips, or the time she and I laughed like fools because a bird flew up her dress and she yelled, "Get it, get it," and I didn't know what to do. They'd remember things like that.

We go along the highway, the lights coming at us like moving spotlights, and I say how it was a good movie and the man in the front seat saying how he sure is hungry, and the woman in the back seat saying she is too, and I say some frozen yogurt sounds good, although I'm still watching the woman in the front seat on account of it being fun, and no one can see where my eyes go in the dark.

The car stops at an open-'til-midnight grocery. I offer to go in with him and the woman sitting next to me says get buttered pecan and I say okay. She says, no, chocolate mint would be better, not the green kind, and if they don't have chocolate mint, the buttered pecan or maybe maple crunch. He says chocolate wouldn't be so bad either, and the car's running, and I say frozen yogurt would be nice, maybe vanilla. The woman sitting next to me says, "I'll go in," and he turns off the engine, and they cross the parking lot, through the doors, toward aisle five, frozen foods and toppings.

The two of us left behind sit in the car and I think I should say something. I swallow hard, say, "Didn't think I'd ever find you," and her eyes do that searchlight thing, and mine do the same, and signals might be going back and forth, but I'm not sure.

"Sometimes, finding is the easy part," she says.

I want to ask what she's talking about, but I think I know.

Then she says, "Did you finish reading . . . ," and we're off talking about books. Easy talking. We read mostly the same ones, call each other and say, do you believe it? Do you believe it? We go on and on, talk about Harry and Catherine, Reese and Ida, Alejandra and John Grady like they're our friends, like they have a life outside those pages.

Inside the open-'til-midnight grocery they line up at the checkout, stack ice cream and toppings on the counter. Between them and us: mostly empty parking lot, windows getting fogged. The engine pings. I clear my throat. She sighs. I wait for words to come out. None do.

The clerk drops food in the bag. I can see that, and the woman in the front sees it too, then hangs her hand on the back of the seat. They're walking toward the automatic door, him carrying the bag of bananas and ice cream and butterscotch topping, her carrying her purse. The hand on the back of the seat, the fingers do a little drum roll.

I take a deep breath, reach forward, put my hand on hers, and she could ask me what do I think I'm doing or pull her hand away or give me a dirty look like I'd better move my hand or get it broken, but instead she turns hers beneath mine so they're face to face, our hands.

They come out the doors and look around the parking lot like they can't remember where the car is and our fingers hang on, squeeze once back and forth, while the man with the bag points, and I can hear him talking and her heels clicking.

Our hands slip apart, go back home. The grocery bag pushes into the car, and they start telling what they found and how they're going to have some pig-out party and how the two of us that stayed in the car shouldn't always be watching what we eat and that we ought to live a little more dangerously.

He starts the car, wipes the breath fog from the window, then gives it gas and swings out of the parking lot.

I lean forward, look out the windshield, take a deep breath, try to see where we're going.

Walt

Below the Surface

I'd heard the argument a hundred times: Mom saying if we were going to build a house, she wanted indoor plumbing, and Dad saying that there wouldn't be enough water. Mom never listened to his logic, how the earth beneath us was honeycombed with coal mines and the ground water seeped out of the wells, down into those tunnels. She never looked at the diagrams Dad drew on the corner of the newspaper with one of the stubby pencils he always carried. "Here, here, look at this, Walt," he'd say, and as much as I wanted to avoid taking sides, I could feel myself being drawn into their disagreement. He'd point to a line on the paper he had labeled Meigs 22 or Kittany 7, tunnels that followed seams of coal far below the surface, and he'd trace the path of water as it seeped deeper and deeper inside the earth. He said there were countless mine shafts that had been sealed off and forgotten. They were everywhere.

Mom would look out the kitchen window and pretend she didn't hear him, but I listened, studied his maps and learned the secrets below the surface. I could name the tunnels, their depth and the direction they ran. I knew where the seams of coal went deeper as they moved east towards the Ohio River, which shafts were subject to cave-ins, where gas leaks were a problem, which tunnels flooded and the spot where the coal car had cut off Mr. Benson's legs. I'd wait for Mom to argue that enough water could be found, but she was always silent. She never put any faith in science, and I knew— if Dad did not—that no amount of logic would ever convince her that a flush toilet would not be possible in our house.

The argument never changed until the night Mom announced Crazy George—she never called him "Crazy" although everyone else in town did—had found water on Petrakis's farm, enough water for indoor plumbing.

"Luck," Dad said. "Flies in the face of common sense."

But I could see that it bothered him, the way he stared over the top of his paper and drummed his fingers on the table.

"George found water for Petrakis, he can find water for us," Mom said.

Dad glanced out the window.

"He's a dowser," Mom said.

Dad shook the newspaper as if Mom's words were a cat he could scare off. "Temporary," he said. "They'll run out sooner or later, more likely sooner."

Crazy George lived on the back road to East Liverpool, out beyond Petrakis's farm and the hill where Mom and Dad hoped to build our house. The grownups whispered about his craziness, about something that he'd done during that Good Friday cave-in; my friends and I thought he was crazy because of the way he talked to his dead wife, going on and on to anyone who listened about how she was buried in the wrong grave. "They made a mistake," he'd say. "They put her over on the side, in someone else's spot." He'd shake his head and ask, "What am I going to do?"

Mom was one of the few who listened to him and was patient while he held up the line at Walton's Grocery or the people coming out of church.

"He did it with a divining rod," she said. "Some people can do that."

"Temporary," Dad repeated.

A week later Mom and I went to Petrakis's farm. Nick Petrakis's wife had died of polio a few years earlier and left him with a daughter to raise. Dad often shook his head and said how tough it would be running a farm with "just a girl." Mom thought Alexie should be around a woman from time to time, and she worried about Alexie and me getting spoiled since we were each an "only child." Mom and I went to the farm often, and each time she'd say we were feeding two birds with one hand.

Alexie was sitting on a hay wagon covered with quarts of strawberries when we arrived. She ran up the drive, and a minute later Nick followed her out of the house. His hair was black as the anthracite coal that came from the mines; his green shirt was open halfway down his chest in a way Mom said was the custom of Greek men.

Nick told Mom he had spoken with George. I raised my eyebrows and whispered to Alexie, "Where's Dorothy? Where's Dorothy?"

"We could ride over, talk to him," Nick said.

Mom suggested Alexie and I wait at the farm—"We don't want to overwhelm George," she said—but we insisted on riding along, eager for a chance to hear Crazy George talk about his dead wife.

While Nick drove, he pointed to a field and said the oats were doing well, pointed to another and said nice clover. The wind coming through the window blew Mom's hair over the back of the seat, and Nick nodded in the same way he had at the fields, said, "You have fine hair, Katy, the color of buckwheat honey." Later, he let his arm hang out the window and said, "Beautiful day."

Nick was different from other men around Unity. Perhaps it was because he spent his days working above ground where he could see the clouds and sun. I'd seen him smash his thumb with a hammer and say no more than *ouch*. He talked to the cows when he milked, and, if one kicked the milk bucket, he'd accuse it of conspiring with the cats. Before Mrs. Petrakis got polio, he sang Greek songs that carried across the fields; sometimes in the middle of one he'd dance across the barn floor or down the drive. He was always telling Mom she looked good or handsome or as bright as a daisy. I laughed when he said those things, but Mom said it would be nice if I picked up a few of his ways.

I usually responded by doing a silly imitation of Nick's dance.

Crazy George was waiting, sitting on his doorstep. Harvey, his skinny, blind-in-one-eye dog, sat beside him.

"My good friend George Abbott," Nick said. "You're looking strong today."

Crazy George scratched his whiskers and looked up at the sky. "Dorothy's buried in the wrong spot," he said.

I bit my lip to keep from laughing, but Mom, Nick and Alexie nodded their heads as if what he had said made perfect sense. Dad would have seen the silliness of it but he wasn't there.

"I'll be next to the wrong person," George said.

Mom nodded.

"I was faithful to Dorothy all my life."

Mom glanced at Nick, then at me, frowning like she didn't want me hearing any of it, afraid of where George's thoughts might be going.

"There wasn't one night the two of us didn't sleep together other than that Good Friday weekend. Forty-three years." He coughed, shook his head. He looked back at his house, then around at the trees.

His voice was scratchy, hard to understand; every time he talked, I cleared my throat. His cheeks were sunken, and, when without his teeth, his face looked as if it might cave in at any moment. His neck was wrinkled and scrawny, and his white hair waved gently in the breeze like the threads of a broken spider web hanging from a tree. He coughed. The bump in his throat jiggled up and down.

"You think I can find you water?" he asked.

"Yes, I do," Mom said, clearly relieved George had changed the subject.

Alexie and I were petting Harvey and trying to peer through the screen door and into his house.

Nick stood with his hands on his hips, his feet set wide apart. He looked ready for a fight but his voice was gentle. "Can you do it, George?"

"Never failed yet." George pushed his lips to the side of his face with the palm of his hand. "I'll teach you," he said to Mom.

"But I thought you could look for us. I can't. I couldn't . . . ."

He held up his hand, "I'll teach you," he repeated.

I wanted to tell Mom it wouldn't work, explain how things were below the surface, but she believed a cricket in the house was good luck, that if you saved the pointed end of a slice of pie until the last bite, a wish would come true, that if you peeled an apple and put the peeling on the windowsill during a full moon, it would curl into the initials of the person you loved; she believed that shooting stars were stars and now she believed a stick could find water.

"What will I owe you?" she asked.

Alexie and I stopped petting Harvey, who smelled pretty bad, and waited.

"Help me move Dorothy," George said.

I knew he was crazy, but the thought of digging in the cemetery late at night made me pray Mom and Nick would go along with it.

"Done," Nick said, and, for a second, he appeared so happy about it all that it looked as if he was going to put his arm around Mom's shoulder and squeeze.

Mom said nothing until we were in the car and on our way back to the farm. "We can't go out there and dig her up. We can't do that," she said.

Nick intentionally took a curve too fast, and Alexie and I slid across the back seat. He looked in the rearview mirror and laughed. "He can't spend eternity next to the wrong person, can he?"

From Mom's silence, we knew she agreed.

After supper, Mom, Dad and I went out to the hill on Middle Ridge Road where Dad was planning to build our house. Dad and I looked for arrowheads in a corner of the field that had recently been plowed while Mom picked wildflowers. Then he carefully counted his steps as he paced off a rectangle, showing me the size of the foundation and where the rooms would be. It seemed as if the house would be small, barely big enough for the three of us, but Dad, reading my thoughts, said that there would be plenty of room. I knew Dad and Mom were eager to get out of the company house and into a place of our own, although they both warned me never to repeat that.

After pointing out where the front and back door would be located, Dad told me things that had happened in the mine that day, the problem with ventilation in a new shaft, a man who'd cracked his ribs. He told me not to tell Mom. "The less she knows about things down there, the better. It'd just make her worry," he said.

Later, while Mom and Dad sat on the blanket talking about the threat of a steel strike and what it would do to the miners, I walked around the field thinking about our digging up Dorothy in the cemetery. Unlike Mom, I had never been afraid of the dark, and strange noises and shadows never spooked me.

Mom stared across the valley at Petrakis's farm. When it appeared as if Dad was about to fall asleep, she asked if he'd put indoor plumbing in the house if she found enough water. "George Abbott is going to show me how," she said.

I moved closer to the blanket, flipped seed heads and pretended not to listen.

"Crazy," Dad murmured.

I didn't know if he was talking about George or Nick or the idea of Mom finding water.

"But what if?" Mom asked.

Dad shook his head. "Two gallons per flush. It's a waste when you have to worry about enough for cooking and drinking."

Mom looked across the small valley. "Nick has indoor plumbing," she said.

Dad glanced at the big white barn in the distance, then looked away as if it was something he didn't want to see. "Luck," he said.

He motioned for me to move closer. "Right, Walter?" I didn't want to answer, but he smiled, punched me in the arm.

"Right?"

"Right," I said.

At dusk, the mosquitoes began biting. Dad blew cigarette smoke over his arms; Mom walked to the top of the hill where she said the breeze kept the bugs away. Dad called up to her, said we'd be going home soon.

"It's hard on women," he whispered.

I nodded although I didn't know what it was that was hard on them.

Dad said the Miller brothers would start building our house soon and that building houses was a clean job and that I should come out and watch, make myself useful. "Be something you might want to do, build houses," he said. "Better than the mines." He blew another puff of smoke on his arms and closed his eyes.

I slipped away, walked up the hill. Mom was staring so intently in the direction of Petrakis's farm that she didn't see me coming. "Boo!" I said.

She jumped and I asked if she was thinking about our new house or Crazy George teaching her to find water.

"Nothing," she said. "I'm thinking about nothing."

I stared at the farm, tried to see what she had been watching.

"I know what you see," I said.

Before I could finish my joke she spun around. "You should learn to leave people alone with their thoughts," she snapped. "You couldn't possibly know what I was thinking."

I shrugged and said that I thought she was trying to see the well or the indoor plumbing. "I was just teasing," I said.

She stared across the valley, and I turned away, began walking to another corner of the field.

"Sorry, Walt." She smiled. "You're right. You're a difficult one to fool."

On the way to the next dowsing lesson, Mom insisted on stopping at the farm to get another basket of strawberries for George. Mom was afraid he wasn't eating right. "He's lonely," she said. Mom wrapped her arms around the steering wheel, got a serious look on her face.

Alexie was working the roadside stand, if you call propping your bare feet up on the trunk of a tree and reading a paperback working.

I sat with her on the back of the wagon, eating strawberries and flipping the stems out into the road, while Mom went up to the house to talk with Nick. We ate an entire quart, sold two, then jumped in the back seat of the car and waited. Nick and Mom eventually came down the drive, talking about plumbing and pumps and pipes. Talk, talk, talk, always talk. Mom would tell him how much she liked the smell of the farm, the plowed fields, the clover. Hmmm, that hay sure smells good, she'd say, and Nick would go on about warm nights, hearing the corn grow, and we have a new calf, a cute fellow, stop in and see it, and, oh I'd love to. On and on until I wanted to bang my head against the side of the car.

Nick pointed at Alexie, told her to behave, winked at me, thanked my mother for the twentieth time, slapped the roof of the car, then stood at the end of the drive and waved. Sometimes I thought he was afraid we'd never bring Alexie back.

Crazy George showed Mom how to walk in circles with a Y-shaped willow branch pointed out in front of her. He'd cut the limb for her from a tree behind his house and said that it wouldn't work for anyone but her. He looked at me when he said it. He adjusted her grip, held her elbows out from her sides.

"I don't know," she said. "I don't know what I'm looking for."

Crazy George stopped, stared at her in surprise. "Sure you do. You know. You know," he whispered, again and again. "You know."

I was embarrassed and couldn't tell if she believed him or not. I worried that people in town might start calling her crazy too.

Mom walked in larger and larger circles and nothing happened. She zigzagged down the drive with Crazy George walking and wheezing behind her. She walked through a flower garden—"My Dorothy planted these," George said—and into the woods. They marched through two fields and back along the fence. Alexie and I stood and stared the way we did when a plane passed overhead. Mom and Crazy George were near the wood pile when she stopped.

"Look, look," she yelled. She was almost dancing.

The stick was pointing straight down. Crazy George laughed and nodded. Mom walked backwards and the stick popped up; she stepped forward and the stick—it looked as if she had no control over it—turned down.

It made no sense. When I was little I'd tap on the pipes of the sliding board out on the playground behind the school, thinking I might be able to signal Dad someplace far below, and for a while I thought I could detect the vibrations of the coal cars rolling on the rails deep beneath the surface. Dad said it wasn't possible, and I soon gave up trying to feel those faint rumbles although it continued to disturb me that many of the women in town claimed they knew the instant there was a cave-in deep in the mines.

"I want to talk with your father," Mom said to Alexie when we turned up the lane to the farm. "Alone," she said, when Alexie and I leaned forward in the seat. We knew she'd tell him about finding water, but I guessed that she also wanted to discuss the digging up of Dorothy without Alexie and me listening in.

Alexie and I ran to the barn where we could stand in one of the stalls and watch from a window. When Nick saw Mom, he stopped the tractor and motioned for her to come with him to a spot near the fence. He knelt down and pointed at the ground. I asked Alexie what was going on, and she said that it was probably a bird, maybe a crow, that when he came to a nest in the field, he'd stare at it, study it as if he'd never seen one before. Then, he'd carefully carry it to the fence where it was safe from the wheels of the tractor and hay wagon.

Alexie petted the baby calf; I watched Mom and Nick, hoped that I could overhear what they were saying about Dorothy. They stood facing each other, his shirt flapping in the breeze, Mom's hair blowing over her shoulder, their heads bobbing up and down, their mouths moving, Nick waving his hands around, acting things out as he talked, but their words didn't reach the barn.

I turned and rubbed the Jersey calf between its big brown eyes with my knuckles.

When I looked outside again, Mom was on the tractor seat, Nick standing behind her on the hitch. They lurched backward and Nick almost fell off. He grabbed the seat, leaned over her shoulder, moved something near the steering wheel, and the tractor lurched forward. They made three large loops around the field. It looked as if Nick was singing.

That night Mom told Dad that George's wife needed to be moved. "I think he's right," Mom said. "He seems to know those things."

"George is loony," Dad said.

Mom looked at me as if I shouldn't hear that sort of thing, which was silly because I'd heard the men coming out of the mines say a lot worse than that. I pretended to read the newspaper. "Nick Petrakis thinks George can find water, and he thinks George might be right about Dorothy," she said.

Dad shook his head. "Nick's a little loony too." Then, looking at me, he asked, "Right?"

I knew it wasn't possible to find water with a stick. Dad had explained how if it were that easy they'd never have trouble staying away from it down in the mines, and I wanted Mom to give up the idea before everyone in town thought she was loony too. Still, I knew indoor plumbing was important to her, and I didn't want to hurt her feelings. "What?" I asked, pretending I hadn't heard the question.

The following week George taught Mom how to distinguish between large reservoirs of water and small seasonal ones. They hiked across fields and along the road while Alexie and I followed quietly at a distance or sat on George's front porch and tried, unsuccessfully, to teach Harvey to fetch.

After each dowsing lesson, we stopped at the farm so Mom could discuss her progress with Nick, and they could make plans for digging up Dorothy. Alexie and I were not allowed to follow them into the fields, where I suspected they discussed George's Craziness, but Mom promised, somewhat reluctantly, that if we behaved and didn't tell anyone, "not a soul," we would be allowed to go to the cemetery, when, as she put it, "things are done."

When Mom eventually took her divining rod to the hill where our house was going to be built, I prayed none of my friends would pass on the road and see her. Dad and I sat on a blanket—we had a square spot where the grass was smashed down from our frequent visits—and watched as she walked around the field, her divining rod pointing in front of her. "Just like gambling," Dad said. He chewed on a blade of grass, then lowered his voice and told me that a water pump had broken and there had been some flooding that day, no one hurt, no damage. He seemed to offer it as evidence of water's fickle nature.

"In Meigs?" I asked.

He nodded, pleased I knew. "But don't tell her," he said. Then he took out a stubby pencil from behind his ear and sketched the floor plans of our house on the corner of the newspaper.

Mom zigzagged back and forth, back and forth. I wanted to call out, ask her to forget it; three cars had passed and I was sure someone had seen her. She was halfway up the hill when the stick pointed down.

"Never seen anyone use a rod that didn't point down somewhere," Dad said. He held out his hands and bent his wrists to show it was a voluntary movement.

Mom corrected her posture, flexed her wrists and crisscrossed the field in the pattern George had taught her. Each pass over the spot, the stick shivered and shook until it pointed at the ground.

"Oh my, it really works," she said. "It really works. Lots of water. Lots." The stick vibrated, shook her hands and threatened to break free of her grasp. She called for me to get some rocks to mark the spot. "Oh my," she said.

Dad walked to where the stick pointed down and began to reach for the willow branch.

"No," she said, holding the forked stick close to her stomach. "It won't work for anyone else."

I dropped three large rocks near Mom's feet. "What do you think of that?" she asked us. "We'll drill here, won't we?"

Dad looked at the stick, glanced around the field carefully as if he were judging distances. He nodded, then went back to the blanket. He had been working twelve hours a day for six straight days; he was tired.

Alexie and I rode to the cemetery in the back of Nick's truck. Mark Davis and Jim Reesh, two high school boys who helped Nick bale hay, sat across from us, three shovels beneath their legs. Mom sat up front, squeezed between Crazy George and Nick, her willow branch safely tucked under the seat. Through the window came the muffled voices of George talking to Dorothy; Mom and Nick talking about corn, weather, and how fate sometimes put people in the wrong places. Mark and Jim peered at us through half-closed eyes as the wind whipped their hair and the shovels bounced and clanged against the bed of the truck.

Reverend Emerick was waiting, one hand clutching a Bible, the other shading his eyes. He looked nervous.

Crazy George was the first out of the truck. He led us across the top of the hill and pointed at a marker.

DOROTHY ABBOTT
May 11, 1897 - August 3, 1956

He shook his head and walked to a new section of the cemetery, pointed to a granite headstone. "She's here," he said.

Reverend Emerick read the marker. "Henry Parsons."

Crazy George got down on one knee, put his hand on the grass. "Nope, it's Dorothy."

Mom pressed closer to the headstone. "What makes you think, when did you . . ."

"I can feel it," he said, holding his hand a few inches above the grass. He motioned for Mom to come beside him, put her palms on the ground.

We all watched while Mom put her hands on the grass as carefully as if she were touching Dorothy's body.

"How?" Mom asked.

Reverend Emerick cleared his throat, looked at a notebook he had taken from his pocket. "Two funerals that day. Mr. Parsons and Mrs. Abbott. Mr. Parsons had no relatives, no one that showed up anyway." He shrugged. "It's never happened before but . . . ." His voice trailed off.

George nodded, shoved his lips around his face. There were coffee stains down the front of his shirt, and he'd forgotten to put a belt in his pants. I felt sorry for him, but I didn't believe Dorothy was in the wrong spot or that he could feel her presence by holding his hand on the ground. I wanted Mom to get off her knees. Things like bodies in the wrong grave and being able to feel a dead person through six feet of dirt didn't happen, and like everyone in town said, he was crazy.

Nick walked back and forth, went to one grave, then the other. "Possible," he said.

Mark and Jim waited by the back of the truck, their arms wrapped around the shovels.

Reverend Emerick, a pale skinny man, unaccustomed to physical labor, said he would pray for guidance and asked us to bow our heads. I knew that I was supposed to be thinking prayer thoughts, but I was embarrassed; I didn't believe this—"hocus pocus," Dad called it—magic below the surface, mysteries that couldn't be explained by a diagram carefully drawn on the corner of a newspaper. A crow called in the field and everyone looked up except the Reverend. Mom and Nick smiled at each other as if it were one of the birds Nick had saved.

"Amen," Reverend Emerick said. He nodded at the boys, indicating they should begin. I wanted to dig too, but Nick shook his head, so Alexie and I sat a few feet away in the shade of a maple and waited.

Reverend Emerick dabbed his forehead, hung his coat on a headstone, and peered into the hole that grew deeper and deeper. From time to time, he glanced nervously toward the road. Large dark wet spots appeared under his arms. I whispered to Alexie that he was going to pass out, and if he did, we'd be stuck with another body.

When the shovels scraped something solid, we all moved closer. The boys stopped while we all looked, then began again, throwing shovels of dirt on the canvas tarp. Eventually, Nick and the Reverend helped them lift the casket out of the ground. They were grunting and groaning as if it weighed a thousand pounds. Crazy George brushed dirt from the wood surface and began to cry. Mom patted him on the back and Nick gripped his arm, but Crazy George said it was all right, he was happy. He said it was Dorothy. "This is her," he said patting the top of the casket. "This is her."

Reverend Emerick and Nick nodded, and I knew then they weren't going to open it, that looking at her wouldn't be necessary. I wanted to ask him how he'd known, how he'd done it. I wanted him to show me the math of it, how you calculated where things were that you couldn't see. I wanted to understand the angles of it, the radar, but I was embarrassed standing there, watching, thinking that I was the only one who didn't know how it was done.

Dad would have said it was luck or that Crazy George had known all along, and if it was that easy, there would never be a problem finding trapped miners.

George put his arm across the casket and made choking noises, while the rest of us looked away. Two hawks floated in a circle over a nearby field and in the distance a clump of clouds appeared to drift in our direction.

After the caskets were lowered into the correct places and Reverend Emerick had said a prayer for each, after the boys had replaced the sod, and the shovels and tarp were back in the truck, we drove George home. Mom asked if he needed anything. He shook his head, said thanks.

"We'll have you over when we get the plumbing in," Mom said.

George waved and went in his house, Harvey following him through the door.

That evening, after supper, Dad, Mom and I went out to our hill; the Miller brothers had started work on our house, and we were eager to see what had been done. There was a large hole in the ground, and some of the grass was torn up from the heavy equipment. Dad inspected the work, showed me where the different rooms would be and explained how the basement walls had to be perfect, "true" he said, or it would throw off the whole house. When he was satisfied, he stretched out on the blanket next to Mom, opened the thermos of lemonade, and squinted at the sky. He said they'd finished the job in Meigs 22, and for the next few days he looked forward to regular hours. Mom said that she wished she'd known Dorothy better.

I asked how Crazy George had known she was in the wrong grave. Dad leaned back on the blanket and closed his eyes. Mom looked at the hole the bulldozer had dug for our house, then stared across the road at Petrakis's farm. For a second I thought she hadn't heard me. "Some people just know," she said.

Her answer troubled me; it had no more logic than apple peelings spelling someone's initials. I was sure she was keeping a secret.

Dad opened his eyes and I waited for him to say it was nonsense, but he pointed at the concrete blocks. "You should come out here and help," he said. "Learn something."

Mom held the divining rod in her hand.

"Can I borrow it?" I asked.

She hesitated, said it was hers, but then nodded.

Dad put his hands behind his head and watched. I was going to do something funny, try to make him laugh, maybe let the stick pull me to the thermos of lemonade or point at one of the clouds. I wanted to make both of them laugh, but Dad's eyes slid shut under the weight of a long day and Mom stared at the stem of a wildflower she twirled between her fingers.

I drifted up the hill, thinking it was all a trick: Mom finding water, Crazy George knowing his wife was in the wrong grave. The divining rod was like a magician's wand, a sleight of hand, a flick of the wrist, nothing more. Mom and Crazy George knew the secret, and they weren't sharing. I studied the ground, looked for a clue that might reveal something deeper.

A breeze carried the clean, sweet smell of fresh cut hay; fireflies flickered like distant carbide lamps; a bullfrog in the creek across the road croaked. The lights went out in Petrakis's barn, and Nick appeared as a tiny figure by the sliding doors. I swung the divining rod back and forth while watching him walk toward the house. The rod began to tug and my fingers tingled. The stick twisted in my hands, shook my arms, pointed across the road.

Then the stick yanked me in a new direction, almost pulled out of my hands. It pointed at Mom, and, as if she felt the accusation it held, she turned and looked at me.

It was too dark to see her expression, but she glanced at Dad, then back at me, "Walt."

I didn't answer. The stick pointed at Petrakis's farm, then back at her. I heard and saw the two of them laughing, Nick singing on the back of the tractor, Nick standing by the car. "Beautiful day, doesn't that hay smell good. That baby crow is a cute one. That moon last night! You have fine hair, Kate." The two of them walking in the fields.

"Walter," she repeated.

"No," I whispered, afraid Dad would wake up and see what I had discovered.

"Walter," she said.

Dad stirred. "We'd better be going," he said.

I didn't move.

Mom stood up and brushed bits of grass and seed off her skirt.

I threw the stick as far as I could, dared her to tell me to pick it up. She watched it land, looked down at the blanket, then up at the stars.

"We're leaving," Dad said.

"No," I repeated.

The frog croaked again in the distance. Dad frowned. "I don't know." There was a mixture of caution and confusion in his voice. He looked at Mom.

"He can walk home if he's careful," Mom said. "He's old enough." She stared at me as if she were trying to put thoughts into my head.

Dad looked back and forth between Mom and me. He said he was glad I was getting attached to the place and not to fall in the hole. "Don't be late," he said.

I walked to the top of the hill, refusing to turn and wave when the car horn honked. "Stupid, stupid woman," I hissed.

I sat on the hill an hour, longer, mumbling nonsense and throwing fistfuls of weeds and grass. I was angry with all of them, Crazy George, Nick, Mom, Dad, Alexie, even Dorothy for being in the wrong grave. I vowed that I'd run away and never return home.

I went to the road and turned towards East Liverpool. I kicked gravel and spit words I'd never used. I walked and ran a mile, two. What was she thinking? What was she doing?

Another hour passed, and I knew Mom and Dad would wonder where I was. Maybe they'd drive back to the hill and look for me. I imagined Mom getting out of the car and calling my name, maybe finding her divining rod. She'd worry and I was glad.

I walked another mile. Soft noises and vague shadows rolled through the trees beyond the fence. A chill went down my spine despite the heat that came off the road. I thought I heard a woman crying.

"Mom," I called, "Mom?" Something moved in the field, but no one answered. I picked up a rock.

I walked around another curve, confused and angry. It was late. I could hear myself breathing and the breeze rustling the leaves. Mom was home, standing at the kitchen sink looking out, waiting for me to come down the road. I knew she was there, fighting back the tears while my dad sat in the other room, nodding off in his chair.

The tree frogs and locusts and crickets were making an awful racket. Somewhere in the distance a dog barked and there was the clang of a bell. I took a few steps and heard a raccoon or cat scurry through the weeds alongside the road. Then I heard something different. A woman crying. I froze. For a few seconds all the other sounds stopped, and I heard only the soft sobbing. I spun around but no one was there.

"Mom," I whispered. "Mom."

I turned, threw rocks at the demons lurking in the shadows and began to run home.

Erratics

Don't like snakes, never did. The one on my desk won't eat and it's beginning to piss me off. Dropped several earthworms in there yesterday, in the terrarium, and the snake jumped back like it was afraid of them, a chicken snake. I dangled a fat, juicy one high above the snake's head, high enough so that it couldn't leap for it and lock onto one of my fingers but low enough so that it might be tempted. I know they eat worms. I remember my friend Alexie feeding them when we were little, making pets of them, milk snakes and black snakes she'd caught in the barn. Even now, with two kids of her own that she's supposed to be setting an example for, she'll pick up a snake, let it twist around her arm while she calls it "Pretty Baby," holds it close to her face, then looks at her son and daughter and says, "Isn't it cute?"

Anyway, I dropped the worm on the snake, figured the dangling and dropping would agitate it a bit, the snake, and it'd eat the worm from anger and hunger, and I wouldn't have to worry about the snake dying, not that it would upset me, the snake going belly up, but it would further damage my reputation here with the kids. The worm landed on the snake's head, crawled over its back, burrowed down in the moss and disappeared. Taunted the snake is what it did.

The kids here are starting to piss me off a bit, too. "Why doesn't the garden snake eat?" "Why doesn't the garden snake eat?"

I shake my head. "Garter snake. Garter with a T as in . . . ." I start to point at Susie Silko's leg, stop. "Garter," I tell them. I don't know why it won't eat; if I did, I'd be a snake doctor. They think because I teach them biology I should know all living things. I majored in geology, go hunting rocks every summer, have boxes and crates of them in the apartment where I live. Ask me about things igneous, sedimentary and metamorphic, things that don't move, I say, but they want to know why the garden snake won't eat.

This morning I went down to the gym looking for a shovel. Usually I'm the first here except for Harley, the custodian. I'm doing my best to make up for all those times I was late last year, my first teaching at this rich private school where the younger kids wear braces and the older ones flash smiles, their teeth snow white, perfect and straight. My lateness to school was, I think, because my body was mostly on Montana time and took many months to adjust. I will tell you more about life in Montana, but first I have to tell you about Harley and what happened in the gym.

Harley and I take turns firing up the coffee pot. He says I make it a bit strong, that one cup gives him the shakes, but I say you can always dilute it with milk or whatever and I hate weak coffee. Harley retired from the railroad ten years ago and still misses the clang of the iron wheels on the track, the lurch of a hundred cars yanked into motion, the mournful wail of the whistle, the rocking of the caboose, the throb of those big diesels, which, he says, you can feel deep in your chest.

Harley has gotten the nickname "Speed" from some sarcastic secretaries and teachers on account of how slow he is to come when he gets the static call on the walkie-talkie he carries in his hip pocket, calls that say Vickie Clark has coughed up her tuna salad lunch in the back of the music room and it is there waiting in the corner for him. Harley comes from Louisiana, where you learn how to pace yourself.

Anyway, I started the coffee—six scoops—went to the gym to look for a shovel, and I heard noises coming from the storeroom, back where they keep the gym and football type equipment. Moaning. Snakes and moaning, two things that scare me. The moaning was pretty strong, and I thought maybe one of the jock football players got hurt, got locked in the storeroom overnight. Somebody's head is going to roll over this, I thought, and for once it isn't going to be mine. I teetered at the door, not wanting to go in, blaming the chicken shit starving snake for my predicament. I didn't want to look inside but knew I had to check it out. Somebody could've been dying.

I opened the door slow, careful, my overactive imagination running wild. Early mornings alone in this big old building, before coffee has sharpened my mind, gives me the creeps. You never know. The groaning grew louder. "Oh, oh, oh," it goes. A woman's voice or a sissy boy in pain. Still, I took it slow, keeping alert to the possibilities of vandalism, robbery or other evil mischief going on and someone lurking in the dark with a football helmet or aluminum baseball bat. I tip-toed over the shoulder pads and water bottles that littered the floor. "Oh, oh," the voice went again.

I looked back in the far corner, behind the tennis nets, soccer stuff and racks of basketballs, and I could see two bodies in the dim light, two mostly naked bodies tangled in the throes of passion, squirming this way and that on the wrestling mat.

I stepped closer and recognized Lou Bigum, our ace number one jock teacher and JV football coach, and I hoped he wasn't back there with one of the bouncy high school girls he's always flexing for—I'd rather see some star fullback holding a knee that's swollen twice the size of a pumpkin than catch a glimpse of Lou clutching a pom-pom girl or a baton twirler. Lou raised himself up a little, not much, and I got a peek of Erika Parsons and I felt such relief that I said, "Whew!" and took another step forward.

Lou had on his sweats, except they were down around his knees, and I couldn't see what Erika had on because the room's only light was coming through the door I'd just opened and Lou being mostly on top of her. Bare legs. I did see bare legs. I stood and stared, not because I wanted to watch or because I couldn't take my eyes off Erika's long legs—she often shows them off in hose as silky smooth as a Siamese cat's back and short skirts that swish back and forth like water in a swinging bucket—but because of this relief I felt and my confusion over what else to do.

I stood there and didn't budge, and Lou was looking at me, and I was looking at him and sneaking peeks at Erika and those legs. Nobody moving.

Erika teaches French, which probably puts extra passion in the blood—the tongue rolling R's, that "H" sound coming from somewhere deep in the throat. After awhile you can no longer fight the hormonal urges and it leads to things like sex.

So I was standing there and they both stopped moving and groaning as if I'd yelled *freeze*, which might have been a pretty funny thing to yell. FREEZE! But I didn't.

Erika turned her head away because she was feeling a little embarrassed maybe, and I felt bad and thought maybe I should tell her what once happened to me and we could all have a big laugh, but I didn't say a word. And Lou didn't move, he stayed there, looking at me and he said, "Christ."

Had I been thinking fast at the time, I'd have said something like, "No, it's me, *Walt*." But you're not thinking at times like that, at least I'm not or I would have yelled "Freeze," so I just said, "I was looking for a shovel."

"Christ," Lou said again. "There aren't any shovels in here."

I nodded, said that my snake, well not really my snake, but the snake on my desk, wouldn't eat, and, as much as I disliked snakes, I didn't wish them harm because it was more fear than dislike, and if I had the shovel, I could go out and maybe dig up some worms, and I wouldn't have to worry about it anymore. "You know where there might be a shovel?" I asked.

Lou said, "Christ, would you close that door?"

I carefully backed my way across the floor, stepping over the tennis net, loose basketballs and other obstacles, swung the door almost shut, and Lou—he hasn't moved, which says something about the strength in those arms, I mean it was like he was in the up push-up position the whole time—hissed for me to get out. "Get out and close the door behind you," he said.

"That's not a high school girl there?" I asked, although I knew it wasn't, I knew it was Erika. If I say something at times like this, it's going to be stupid, even when I try hard for it not to be.

Lou stared at me. "No," he said and lots of breath came out when he said it, like he couldn't hold himself in that position much longer.

I nodded, "You come on up to my room and see the snake," I said. "You too, Erika," I whispered.

I quietly closed the door, hustled back to the boiler room and had a cup of just-perked-six-scoop-coffee with Harley. Mornings that start off like this you could probably forget the coffee.

I didn't mention it to Harley, the moans or what I saw, but it hung in my mind, the bare smooth legs of a woman.

This private school is in Moreland Hills, a Cleveland suburb. Lots of money. Money coming out the kazoo. The kids here drive their own cars, mostly imported and red, park them in the school lot, sashay up the sidewalk wearing ninety-dollar sunglasses (No, I wouldn't have believed it either) and eighty-dollar jeans with labels they leave on and flaunt a few inches above their behinds. It's a different world.

Where I'm from most recently is Montana, which seems a whole lot farther away than the thirty-hour drive it took to get here. Sweet Grass County. Just east of the Crazy Mountains, fifty miles north of Granite Peak, highest place in the state at over twelve thousand feet. I went to college in Billings, got a degree in geology and a teaching certificate which I used on the Crow Indian Reservation south of town. The Indian kids didn't wear eighty-dollar jeans or ninety-dollar sunglasses and they drove banged up trucks with bald tires, but if you told'm it was a garter snake, they would have spelled it with a T.

In the summers I'd drive my pickup into the mountains, The Crazies or the Big Belts—you go to Montana you've got to see the Big Belts, I mean take an extra two days, two weeks, whatever, but get your ass out of the car and hike up the trails, press your face in the bear grass blossoms. Yellow powder will stick to your nose and all day you will smile and dream feel-good thoughts. I'd pull off the road, then ride Logan up into those hard to get to places, government land mostly, and for a week at a time it was me, the horse and the sweet smell of bear grass. Eat when hungry, sleep when tired, read a book, soak up the stars and sky all around you.

I'd collect rocks, sort of prospecting, except I'd fill the saddle bags, ride back to the truck, dump the rocks in the bed and go back looking for more. I found garnet and copper—if you don't call it Big Sky Country, you call it the Copper State—and galena crystals as big as your fist, looking like broken mirrors. You could call it the Lead State too, if you wanted. Near Pine Creek I found rose quartz, agates and jasper. I'd fill up the back of the truck, all the time sucking up the thin, cool air out of that big, beautiful, blue sky. I'd keep some of the rocks, the moss agates being my favorites, and take the rest over to the tourist shops in Billings, Bozeman and Missoula.

Some here ask if I didn't get tired of that, lonely. I say, no, but you can see them waiting for more.

I can't explain.

You get lots of questions when you're in a new place and most people mean well by them. One thing I always get asked is how did I end up here in Ohio.

Ohio is where I started.

My father died shortly after retiring from the coal mine and my mother was alone, and I worried. I thought I'd better come back to Ohio, be close even though she said she would be "fine, fine, fine."

I sensed a lack of conviction in the way she said, "fine, fine, fine," and I had this huge guilt: me being so happy out there in the mountains and her back here being lonely and forty-seven years old. I felt guilty about not being with my dad and not writing and calling more often.

So I came back and am now only an hour drive from my mother, who last month started dating a neighbor, a man who just happens to be the father of one of my childhood friends. And now she feels guilty about dating someone who isn't my father, so if this wasn't a story about a hungry snake it could be a story about guilt.

Anyway, one thing led to another as they often do, and the school here liked the part where I said I had been a geologist in Montana and had taught on a reservation, so I was hired. The power of B.S.

My life.

I want to tell Harley about the moaning and groaning, the sex in the storeroom, but he grins in a way that makes me think he already knows. Don't think I talk like this in front of the kids, swearing and saying sex and all that. Once or twice, maybe, by mistake, when I get tongue-tied or confused. Like last week. I was teaching simple machines. In the back row, Chuck Dolan, sixteen-carat gold chain as big as a dog collar around his neck, gold rings in his ears. Chuck, who drives around the school parking lot, three, four times every morning in his new Dodge Ram pickup waving the Confederate flag from his window and yelling what he thinks might be a Rebel yell. Chuck being too ignorant to know Ohio is Yankee land. Chuck was dozing, drool dripping from the corner of his mouth. I was on levers, how they can lift loads and all that and getting mighty peeved that he had it so soft and had no desire to improve himself. I was thinking: "Where's the fulcrum, Chuck?" But what I said was, "Where's the chulcrum, Fuck?"

So I'm drinking coffee with Harley, wondering how I'm going to get a shovel.

Remember the snake? I think if I dig deeper, I might be able to get the bigger worms, the truly juicy ones, the gourmet wigglers. People here who worm fish—in Montana it's all flies—prefer the fat ones, maybe the snake will too. I ask Harley and he agrees. He says there are shovels under the football bleachers, so we go out there together and find them and start digging.

Nothing. We dig under the bleachers and beside the ticket booth. Nothing. It's like the worms knew ahead of time they'd be tossed to a hunger-crazed snake and they've all left. I start getting warm and pull off my tie, which I don't like to wear anyway, and it all makes me angry with the snake. "How about over by the refreshment stand, next to the senior rock?" says Harley. He explains how the football booster moms throw coffee grounds out the back door after the games and that worms like that.

We go there and right off get a half dozen giant juicy ones, squirming and wiggling from all that caffeine. Makes you wonder, doesn't it? I mean, Harley is the custodian and I'm the biology teacher, and he's showing me where to dig up worms.

Let me tell you about the rock, the senior rock, the one by the refreshment stand.

First time I saw it was last year. I was walking around the football field and there it was. A boulder as big as a Buick, covered with white paint and blue letters that said, "Seniors Rule." I studied the rock, scraped off a bit of paint with my pocket knife. Granite. Big chunks of granite don't belong here. The Ice Age glacier scooped them up from places far north, smuggled them south, hidden in all that frozen water until the big thaw ten thousand years ago, then dropped them.

I took pictures. I brought my classes outside to show them, scraped off more paint so they could see the granite, the tiny crystals of mica and quartz. I talked about the sheets of ice and pointed up at the low crawling clouds above our heads where the top of the glacier once was. I told them how it made me feel tiny and temporary, how time was not to be whittled away. We are not rocks, I said.

The students looked elsewhere, talked about their sunglasses and cars, the CD's they carried in their book bags and what they wanted to write on the rock. Joyce Roland complained that I was not teaching them biology.

Every class, same thing. I told them to behave, not to instigate any silliness that would reflect poorly on themselves, their families or the United States of America. I worked myself up, said that the rock didn't belong in our neck of the woods, that it came from Canada. I told them to think how it was stuck for maybe a hundred thousand years inside some glacier before it fell free, only to find itself a thousand miles from home. "Maybe we should take it back," I said.

In the afternoon the art teacher with red hair was out there with her students, and they were all drawing clouds and trees and whatever except for the art teacher, who was drawing the rock. I was telling my classes the part about how the rock dropped out of a glacier, and this art teacher with red hair, Marsha was her name, smiled, and I smiled back as she was one of the only ones to appreciate the wonder of it all. Marsha's dress whipped in the breeze, and I was careful not to look as that might be mistaken for foxy eyes, which Mr. Moore warned the male teachers the first day of school not to have.

"Look, look," I said to the students, trying to stir up enthusiasm, "sit on the rock, here, sit. Say 'erratic.'" But the students played grab-ass games and whispered about the party at Mark Leonard's, whose parents were going to be away that weekend.

Marsha the artist put down her pad and pencils and climbed up beside me. She was tall and thin, and her feet dangled over the side of the rock almost as far as mine. She wedged her dress down between her legs with the side of her hand to stop its flapping in the breeze, then looked up at the clouds. "A long way to fall," she said.

The two of us sat on the rock, talked about that long ago giant sheet of ice and stared up at sky where the top of the glacier once was.

"We are not rocks," I said.

She grinned, stretched her legs out in front of her. "I'm not," she answered.

After school that day I got a pink "see-me" note from Mr. Moore, our ace number one principal. I thought he'd like hearing about this rock, maybe even change the school mascot to the "Erratics," which described the football team a whole lot better than "Beavers." I thought he'd be pleased that I took the students outside although some were screwing around, playing games and yelling back at the kids who were leaning out the windows of the building. But he said that I was seen scratching paint off the senior rock. "The rock is a tradition here," he said.

"Ten thousand years," I answered.

He squinted. "Only seniors paint it. Don't be scraping their slogans off the rock, and, if you take your classes outside again, get my approval first."

I came back to school late that night and painted the rock, wrote on it, "I want to go home." Get it? The rock wants to go home. Back to Canada. Ten thousand years is a long time to be away. Every day for a week I saw that rock and what I wrote on it and I laughed every time. Gosh, it was funny. I laugh now, just thinking about it. "I want to go home."

Anyway. It was like a big mystery who wrote on the rock and no one could figure it out except for this red-head Marsha artist-teacher who wedged her dress between her legs when she was sitting next to me on the rock. She gave me the look and nod when she walked by my door. "Nice art work," she whispered, which I pretended not to understand.

Then this Marsha, who I was beginning to like, said she knew some woods where you climb a big hill and from the top you can see all of downtown Cleveland and Lake Erie, and there are wild turkeys and flying squirrels and almost no one knows about it, would I like to go? So the two of us went.

Nothing funny going on. We went back almost every week, just talking and watching for those turkeys and flying squirrels, which we never did see. We joked about maybe taking the rock back to Canada, too. I figured the cost of renting a flatbed truck and some crane to hoist it aboard. Marsha talked about how she'd fix a picnic lunch for us to eat on the way and would fried chicken be okay with me. She said we'd have to sneak in late at night to pick up the rock, and I would say, "Yes, yes, that sounds good."

Sometimes we'd get so carried away that I thought we'd really do it. Marsha said by the time we got it back to the Canadian Shield another ice age would probably come and carry that rock back to Ohio. I said we'd pick it up and truck that rock north again. Just silliness, that's all.

But I should tell you the rest since I already told you about Lou and Erika, although this is not going to be the same thing. Well, to an extent it is.

One time Marsha and I were walking there in the woods, the sway of her hips doing erotic hypnotic things to my mind and body parts. (It was like smelling Bear Grass.) We talked small talk and our plans for the rock. I didn't pay much attention to what I said—at times my jaw gets loose and goes on and on without much help from my brain. I was like that for some time, yakking away, watching the sky and the clouds and her shadow on the narrow dirt path.

It was spring, which, like talking French, can do things to a person, and for no reason at all she stopped, and I stopped, and we looked at each other up and down the face, giving extra time to the eyes and lips.

In no time at all we were sitting on a soft spot of grass, hugging, kissing, and groping. My ears hummed. I put my nose in her hair and breathed deep of that smell that was almost as good as bear grass and it was then, when the buttons were being undone and I was trying to locate the fastener on the back of her bra that I heard whistling.

Whistling. An old couple hiking. He had on this huge hat, and she wore a sweatshirt tied around her waist, and they walked by like watching two people hug and kiss and pull their clothes off on the grass was something they see everyday. "Afternoon," he said.

And get this: Marsha and I said, "Afternoon."

It, the whistling and the "good afternoon," stopped the progress of our undressing and groping and gave my brain and brakes a second. Gave Marsha's time too.

We sucked in deep gulps of air, went "Whew!" re-did our buttons and tucked ourselves back in. That was when Marsha dropped the bomb that she wanted to move to the city, to Cleveland. "A better place for an artist," she said, brushing the grass from the seat of her jeans. I was shook up and confused, had heard that some people preferred living in cities but wasn't sure why. "I have a horse," I said.

On the way home, Marsha leaned over and whispered, her breath as warm and soft on my neck as a June breeze in the Big Belt Mountains. "It's on the front."

"The front?" I said.

She tapped her chest, then her fingers did the motion of unfastening her bra.

I nodded, worked hard at keeping the truck on the road.

Anyway, back to the snake, which it seems like I forgot but I didn't. I carry the worms to my room in one of the empty coffee cans we have sitting down there in the boiler room, and Harley says he'll be up later to see if the snake eats them, but I know it's going to be awhile before he gets there. Erika Parsons passes me in the hall, turns red, but tries to act normal. I say, "Morning," and move on as if nothing happened. I can do that.

I walk the halls between classes and smile at the kids, thank them for coming and say, "Hey, hey," when I see them doing things they aren't supposed to do. The kids smile like we share a secret, but I don't know what it is. I want to go up to them and say, What? What? But I don't. I nod, pretend I understand.

Another thing Mr. Moore said is one of my problems is roaming the halls during class time. There's a letter in my file about it.

The problem is I've got a room without windows. Can you believe it? Every once in a while I've got to see what it looks like outside. Don't forget, I took the course. Meteorology 201: Cumulonimbus clouds at three thousand feet, towering up to thirty, approaching at thirty-five miles per hour. Watch out! Rain, heavy at times. Thunder, lightning, possible hail. Clear and cool tomorrow.

And I have a room without windows.

So.

I teach the rest of the day, stay in my room and don't roam. I write on the board, notes about photosynthesis and respiration, which isn't too bad because it involves chemicals and chemicals are a little like rocks. Except I have trouble concentrating because my mind sometimes flashes to Erika's legs and sometimes it flashes to Marsha's up-front bra fastener, which happened nearly six months ago and I shouldn't still be thinking about but do because I just finished mentioning it.

Harley comes up to my room at the end of the day. We open the worm can and they look okay because of the dirt and grass we put in there with them. The snake is curled up next to a squirrel skull I found when I was out walking. Harley and I watch the snake, Harley on one side of the terrarium, me on the other. "Doesn't look happy," he says, which sounds silly because I wouldn't know a happy snake if I saw one, but Harley says it and I agree.

"What's the problem?" I ask.

Harley shakes his head, rubs his chin. "When I was with the railroad, there'd be snakes sunning themselves on the rails in the spring. Black snakes and rattlers. Some six foot long. Out there trying to warm themselves up." Harley shakes his head again. "Some of the smart ones could feel the trains coming and would slither off, but others . . . ." He winces.

We both look in the terrarium at the garter snake. "It's not right," he says, "keeping an animal caged up like this. Kids want to see a snake, they should go outside, look for one."

It makes sense, and I think again how much Harley knows his biology and other things, and for a second I almost tell him about the moans in the storeroom. "Turn it loose?"

"We can try the worms," he says, "since we've got them, but letting it go would be best."

"You carry it?" I ask.

He nods, reaches into the terrarium, lifts it out. The snake shows lots of life, the tail whipping back and forth, but Harley has a good grip, and we walk down the hall, out the gym doors toward the concession stand and beyond the end of the football field.

Most of the fancy red cars are gone, the parking lot almost empty. Everyone on their way to the places they're going. The sun low in the pale Ohio sky.

Harley puts the snake down near the goalpost and it wiggles off. "It'll be okay," he says.

We stand and watch the snake slither through the grass. Soon it will be visiting other snakes or getting fat on worms, maybe finding a snake hole it can call its own. Had it good in the cage, though. Warm, plenty of food, no dogs or cats pouncing on it. You never know.

We're walking toward the rock and it seems like a good spot to stop and rest, fill Harley in on the events of the day. "Want to sit?" I ask.

He nods, and we climb over the latest senior slogan: "Homecoming '76," and we sit on the rock, look up at a silver dot, a jet, passing high overhead. Behind us, one of the last cars in the parking lot peels out, spraying gravel across the asphalt. Harley slaps his knee and says, "Well."

But I don't move. I study the sky and imagine all that ice melting, boulders the size of big league ball fields falling to earth. And water! The water pouring off the top of that ice sheet, down through the soft spots, must have been something. I can hear the thunderous crash of ten ton rocks striking the ground, smashing other rocks; the roar of water tumbling thousands of feet, cold rivers carving their way through the ice, gurgling over bumps and around curves. I can hear the soft drip of icicles, the squawk of gulls, the flap of wings, the thump, thump of hearts, the sounds we make when trying to find our way home.

Lines

Vick has enthusiasm, a sense of humor and can talk geology for hours: volcanic glass, igneous intrusions, how the greatest turbulence occurs where two rivers come together. When we're alone on our way to the quarry she calls me Walt. She's seventeen and has pretty lips.

The quarries are across the line in Pennsylvania. Those of us living in Unity, Ohio, never say, "Pennsylvania." We say, "Pee-ay." Many here say it with a tone, an attitude, the way they might greet a cheap-suited stranger standing at their door carrying a briefcase and a fake smile. They don't like the Pee-ay fraternity kids sneaking into Ohio late at night to steal the town signs or the way problems and affairs that brew in the Brown Jug Bar and the Lucky Leaf Motel out on Route 14 frequently boil over into the streets and bedrooms of Unity. Most people here would avoid Pee-ay entirely if they could, although a few go shopping in Beaver Falls or Sharon— no sales tax—but they will not buy milk there, not medicine, nothing like that.

Three years ago Billy Lange (both his mother and father were former students of mine) missed a curve on the back road to New Darlington and crashed his '83 red Trans Am into a tree. A steady stream of the curious and the morbid went there the days after the accident, stared at the skid marks, kicked at the pieces of broken glass, then came back to town and whispered about the red paint on the tree trunk and whether Billy had died quickly or not.

The Pee-ay State Police estimated Billy's speed at over eighty, but many on this side of the line blamed the accident on Pee-ay, the way the road twists and turns, sometimes comes around until it almost crosses itself.

Since they've finished I-60 to Sharon, the back road is mostly deserted except for those of us going to the quarry, the Billy Langes racing their cars and couples looking for a place to be alone.

Unity is small. Two thousand people, maybe less. When Laura and I started seeing each other three years ago, friends and neighbors were happy, said she'd be good for me, and that we'd been alone long enough. Arnold had his heart attack while he and Laura were eating at Bernoulli's—something people still discuss while waiting for their pizza to come out of the oven. No warning. Dead when he hit the floor. I'd been divorced for five years, long enough to regain some lost respectability, so it wasn't surprising that, after a period of time and a couple of Sundays sharing the pew at church, some eventually tried to pair us up.

Laura's the nurse at the Lester Edison School for handicapped kids. In the evenings, she visits old ladies, gives them B-12 shots, takes their blood pressure and holds their hands. Laura says that I think too much, life is simple and I should not make it difficult. She reads books that explain why we are the way we are, what planets we are from and what we must do to avoid a life of guilt and misery. "You're in chapter four," she says, when I sit on the front porch until midnight because the news has made me sad. "Chapter eight," she says when I talk too much about Vick.

Although I sometimes collect the offering at the First Methodist Church, and, in September, I was elected president of the Rotary Club, a position not normally held by a teacher, a position I did not want, I don't hold a candle to Laura when it comes to goodness. Laura sends out a hundred Christmas cards, more, signs each one, "Love, Laura." She's a saint. That's what people say. Still, some boldly remind us that we're not getting younger and ask if we have plans.

Vick wants to be a geologist.

The quarries shouldn't be there. Limestone is western Ohio, Indiana. Not Pennsylvania. When I mention this to Laura over coffee, she makes a joke about it and says, "Everything in Pee-ay's a mistake."

But Vick and I don't think so.

We go there on the weekends, cross the Pee-ay line, sometimes alone, sometimes with students and parents. We dig and scrape, find fossils. Brachiopods mostly, but ammonites too. No one can find them like Vick. She has a sixth sense about it. I can't find them like she can and I've been doing it for years.

The parents are kind and thank me for taking time with the kids, but what else do I have to do except ride my bike, and I can only go so far.

Besides.

Vick's been accepted at the University of Montana—I wrote a recommendation, said how she has wings and is going to fly. She's waiting to hear about a scholarship. Vick decided on the U. of M. because of the great geology department, the mountain behind the bookstore, and the stories I told her from when I once lived in that Big Sky state.

Still, Montana is a long way from Unity even if the road getting there is pretty straight.

The teachers at school call Vick my partner and tease that she should get part of my paycheck for all the help she is. Because of her work at the quarry, our high school now has a collection of fossils better than any other in the state. There have been articles in the *Youngstown Vindicator* about the collection along with pictures of Vick and me beside the display. Saturday morning, Ace and Denny buy me coffee at Huck's, slap me on the back and say how it was a good picture.

Ace says, "Pretty girl, isn't she?" Ace owns a store in town that sells cigarettes, jocks and Hallmark Cards.

I say she is, then quickly tell them that she can read topo maps, discuss stream turbidity and glacial history and how in the middle of looking for fossils she might do a cartwheel or dive in the quarry and swim even though the water is black with cold.

Another thing they ask is who Vick dates. I say I don't know, that we only talk about rocks; Ace nods and says, "Pretty girl."

Denny says, "Rodney Cole. She dates Rodney Cole."

I nod as if I just remembered. "She doesn't have pierced ears," I say, wondering even as I say it why I do.

Ace shakes his head, eats his donut; Denny stares at me over his coffee.

Vick and I meet at the high school and she slides into my car, smiles. She has a wide mouth, pretty teeth, an expressive face. "Walt," she says, her lips looking as if they're going to whistle or pucker every time she says my name. Then she holds out her can of Cherry Pepsi. "Sip?" she asks.

I shake my head but she pushes the can closer. "It's good."

I take the can, a red smudge on top, sip, hunch over the wheel, take the curves nice and gentle, fizz and cherry and lipstick taste on my tongue.

No one in town knows for sure where you cross into Pee-ay. We argue about it. Some think Landsberger's farm is on the Ohio side of the line, but others say, no, that the farm—the barn, the milk storage tank to be exact—straddles the line, and still others think you don't hit Pee-ay until just before the curve where Billy Lange smashed into the tree. There are no markers, no signs, no changes in the pavement that would give you a clue. On Route 14, a big green sign welcomes you into Pennsylvania, but out here on the back road there's nothing.

Vick and I make jokes about where the line is, sometimes pretend we can see it as we go down the road, but we don't know, not really.

We pass the Pepsi back and forth, a warm breeze blows in the window. She kicks off her sandals, pulls up her legs, puts her bare feet on the dash, and we pass the next few miles with only the pop can and an occasional grin going back and forth between us.

Ace is building a scuba shop at the quarry and has been out working every weekend. Two professors from Youngstown University have been there and a Ph.D. from Akron, but today our car is the only one.

"Ready?" I say and she nods, opens the door and we head out, follow a narrow ledge around the quarry. Although we're alone, we whisper, and our words go out across the water, bounce against the rocks on the other side and come back to us.

At first the Ph.Ds talked to Vick as if she knew nothing. They didn't even say Devonian or Permian, and they called the trilobite fossils little critters instead of extinct arthropods. It made me angry. Then they found out how much she knew and they were impressed, but they didn't ask her opinion on things, why the limestone is here in the first place.

Hunting fossils, looking real close, wanting to find them in the worst way, makes my eyes go buggy, things blur. I look away, try to focus. It's April. A breeze makes ripples on the water, and, from time to time, I glimpse something moving beneath the surface.

We sit on a rock, take off sandals and boots, slip our feet in the water. I'm embarrassed by my toes, which are crooked and point in the wrong direction.

"Cute toes," Vick says, and I wiggle them although they are stiff with cold. Then I look at hers, at her toenails, which she has painted bright red.

"Yours too," I answer.

Clouds crawl across the sky, and we see things in them, a turtle, a cow, a castle.

On Fridays, Vick stops in my room after school and we drink coffee, look at the fossils we've found, trade rocks, talk about her going to school. We tinker on a seismograph we have been building, hope for an earthquake, just a little one, when it's done. The door to the room always open, the lights always on.

Murray, whose room is across the hall from mine, and Cheryl, who teaches French, stop to ask what's so funny, say they can hear us laughing down the hall. We shrug and they look at the fossils on the table, pick them up, turn them over and ask questions. How old are they? What's this one called? Are they hard to find? Vick answers, shows them how we clean the brachiopods and invites them to pull up a chair and join us. They say it sounds like fun, hunting fossils, and that they want to go to the quarry sometime. We say sure, and they leave, call back to us from down the hall, tell us to have a good weekend.

Vick holds up a fossil and says that she can't imagine six hundred million years. I say I can't imagine it either. I tell her that I sit on my front steps at night and stare at the stars or listen to the rain until after midnight, trying to understand things. I say that it keeps me awake. I mean it as a joke although it's true. Vick blushes and I think I've said something I shouldn't, but then we play a game of saying a period of time we can't imagine. Six million years, six hundred thousand, a thousand. We get down to six years and Vick looks at the clock, "Six minutes," she says.

The following Monday there is a headline in the *Vindicator* about Lou Bigum, a high school physical education teacher in a private school up near Cleveland where I used to teach, who is accused of having had a sexual relationship with one of the students. I knew him years ago, but I don't tell anyone. His name and picture are on the front page, and it's the big story on the local evening news.

Both the article and the news anchor on Channel Five say that Bigum has been suspended from his job and that he will be fired if the allegations are true. Criminal charges are also possible. The girl's name is not being released. She's sixteen.

I can't get it out of my mind. I wonder all sorts of things. Who turned him in? The girl? Her parents? Someone at school? Were they caught together on school grounds or hiding somewhere on a back road? I resent Bigum and what he's done and the newspaper for putting it on the front page, and I can't sleep for wondering how it happened.

The teachers talk about it at lunch all week. Even Murray, who usually wants to talk baseball and spring training, stops in my room after school and in the middle of saying how the Indians need a starting pitcher asks if I think maybe Vick has a crush on me. "Feelings" is the word he uses. "You think there's a chance Vick has feelings for you?" he asks.

I can't answer for a second, then I act surprised, then I say, "No!" shake my head as if it isn't even a possibility. "We talk about rocks," I say, "and besides, she knows . . . ," but I don't know how to finish the sentence, so I shake my head again, "No."

Murray nods, but later in the week, when he and Cheryl are passing the room after school and Vick and I are sitting at the desk looking at fossils, they don't stop, don't say, "Have a good weekend."

Over Easter vacation some of the students and parents have a party at the quarry—Unity is not a wealthy town and despite the urge to go south over spring vacation, few do. There's a campfire with hot dogs and marshmallows and coolers full of pop. It's Vick's birthday and someone has brought a cake. Laura made chocolate chip cookies for the kids and fat free brownies for the rest of us. She talks with the parents, asks about broken bones, heart palpitations, blood pressure, relatives recently in or out of the hospital and her theories on what appears to be a surprisingly high incidence of gout in Unity.

We sit on logs and I worry about one of the kids getting silly and falling into the water, which no one does although from time to time someone throws a rock in that direction, and we all stop talking and listen when it goes plunk.

Everyone sings happy birthday to Vick, and we all get a little square of chocolate cake. I want to give her a geode. I've tied a ribbon around it and have it hidden in the cooler, but there's too many people around, and I decide to wait until later. Rodney flirts with her, asks if she's wearing her red swimsuit, and when she says, "No," he dares her to prove it.

Rodney and a couple of the parents glance at me as if I might have something to say, but I don't. Laura has her arm on my shoulder. Sparks swirl up from the fire. I sit too close to the flames and almost burn my face.

I found the geode in a dry river bed near Rattlesnake Mountain, Utah. I'd been looking for garnets without much success, when I stumbled on a brown rock about the size and shape of a softball. I looked at it a dozen times before it registered. I picked it up, rolled it over, hefted it in one hand, then the other. I'd been thinking garnet all day long and couldn't even get geode in my mind, but there it was. It was the first one I ever found, and I shouted although no one was around to hear.

At the senior breakfast Vick and I are seated next to each other, which is not our doing. A small earthquake shakes northeast Ohio the very week we finish the seismograph. You know, things like that happen.

Sometimes I open my desk drawer after lunch and find a peppermint, a Tootsie Roll, once a Clark Bar, my favorite.

Vick is at the quarry with her parents Saturday afternoon when I stop to look. Her mom, 'Cille, asks about Laura, how is she doing at Lester Edison with all the kids, and says thank goodness for people like her and be sure to tell her hello.

Vick's father doesn't say anything. Maybe a bad day, maybe something else.

Vick says her parents have to go pick her brother up from baseball practice, and she wants to hunt fossils a little longer, so would I mind dropping her off at her house if I'm going that way in a little while? I say sure, I don't mind taking her home. I say I don't mind at all.

Vick's mother, 'Cille, says, "Are you sure?"

I say, "Not at all," but Vick's father says that she's looked around enough for today and that she has work to do.

"We'll take her home," he says.

I expect Vick to argue but she doesn't. She smiles and thanks me for offering to take her home and warns me to leave some fossils for her to find. She waves as the car crunches out the gravel drive and heads back to town.

A week later, Vick knocks on my front door, which is a big surprise. "This is a surprise," I say, and she points at the plate of cookies she's holding. The cookies are in the shapes of fossils: trilobites, ammonites, brachiopods, even a fern fossil cookie that vaguely resembles a Christmas tree.

We teeter in the doorway. The incident between the physical education teacher and the student at the private school troubles me still. An ugly thing. I try not to read or listen to the news about it, but there's talk almost every day in the lounge.

It's not good taking advantage of someone. Sixteen, seventeen, eighteen. So young.

Goose bumps dot her arm and it's hard not to touch them, try to smooth them out, but, of course, I don't. Years ago when I was teaching at the private school, Sara Bacon, who was a senior at the time, came to my room after school and asked me to feel her leg. "Here," she said, pointing to a spot about halfway up her thigh, her leg long, tan, and smooth. It was September and she was wearing shorts, which the kids were allowed to do the first and last grading period.

"I can't," I said.

"No, no," she said. "Really. Feel right here." She put her foot on the seat of a chair, reached for my hand and leaned her leg in my direction. "I got hit in gym class, feels like there's a big knot in there." She tried again to grab my hand, but I didn't, wouldn't touch.

Vick raises her eyebrows. "Try one," she says, pushing the plate of cookies closer. The breeze blows a strand of hair into her mouth and she puffs it out.

My hand hovers over the plate. "Want to come in and have one?" I ask.

She says that she's eaten a dozen and if she eats one more she'll die, then steps inside. She looks around the room, checks out the place where I live.

"Good news," she says, opening her eyes wide, waiting for my response.

"Good news?" I ask.

She pulls an envelope out of her hip pocket.

It says that Montana University has given her a scholarship. "Vick!" I say, and we almost hug we're so excited, but at the last minute I pat her on the back and she touches my shoulder.

We eat cookies, drink milk. She thanks me for writing the letter. We sit and stare out the window at the cows across the road. I can feel something in the room with us but I don't know what it is. The cows munch their way across the field while we talk about Montana, the quarry and how the little cactus on the windowsill doesn't look too good. Vick takes our glasses to the sink, rinses them, says she better go.

I follow her to the door, thank her for the cookies and say how I enjoyed the visit. Walking across the porch, she stops, turns. "You worry too much," she says, then grins and skips down the steps and to her car.

But I do worry. I have dreams, unthinkable thoughts. For Christsakes, I'm fifty-two almost. I look even older.

Lou Bigum is married. He's been fired and is waiting trial. People in town talk about his evilness and shake their heads about how something like that could happen. They scrutinize the teachers in our school, try to guess if there is a Lou among us.

On Memorial Day, I pick up Laura—we do not live together, although at times, if it's raining, cold or late, she will sleep over (her car parked in my garage so students can't see)—and we go to her sister's for a family cookout.

A dozen of us sit on the just-finished backyard deck, breathe in charcoal smoke and hamburger smells, sip the lemonade cold and sweet, white winter legs poking out of our shorts. There is talk about Disney World and some say that Laura and I must go there and everyone nods, but my mind drifts, runs elsewhere. Twice I'm asked if I'm okay, if something is wrong.

I feel guilty because of the worried looks Laura gives me. I compliment the hamburgers and ask about Disney World, how long it took to get there and where to stay and what they liked best, but I don't hear the answers, and I don't think it's any place I care to visit.

Montana would be interesting. It would be fun to drive Vick there, although I realize what a ridiculous idea that is. I mean it would be fun to see the university again, and we could talk the entire way, forty hours of roadside geology, and we wouldn't worry about the time or when Vick needed to get home.

During the summer, Vick works at the library. Her hours are odd, some mornings, some evenings, and weekends. We juggle our trips to the quarry between her work schedule and our other obligations. Laura says that Vick has a father fixation on me and I should be careful. She says that I am vulnerable, and I can read about it in one of her books. "Invite Rodney to the quarry when you go," she says, but I don't. Laura thinks people might get the wrong idea if they see Vick and me—just the two of us—"over there," so she sometimes goes along, sits on a rock in the shade and watches while Vick and I hunt fossils. She reads a book and will ask if we've found anything and tell us that if we have, she wants to see it. On days when Ace is working on his scuba shop, Laura will walk over and visit, watch him pound nails and cut boards.

Vick doesn't do cartwheels with Laura there, although she once threw a small rock at me. On the way home, when we pass Landsberger's farm, Laura will give a big sigh, say how good it is to be back in Ohio.

The end of August, the entire summer gone, Vick packing, getting ready to go. I want to see her one more time, do our quarry thing, but she's not at the library the two days I pick up and drop off books, and I worry that if I call, her father or mother might answer the phone and ask what do I want.

But I call anyway and when the phone rings Vick answers and I say, "This is Walt."

She laughs and says, "Walt."

I say that I'm going over to the quarries and know she is probably busy packing but was wondering if she might want to ride along, go there one last time. It comes out too fast, like I'm out of breath or someone has a gun to my head.

Vick wants to know what time.

"Now," I say, embarrassed. I start to add that we can go later if that is better and that I can pick her up or meet her at school.

"I'm ready," she answers.

On the way to the quarry, as we pass Landsberger's farm, Vick tells me that when she was studying earthquakes on her own back in the ninth grade she misread *subduction zone*. She thought it said *seduction* zone. She points to a weed-lined dirt road ahead that disappears into some trees and says, "Every time we pass that road I think, 'seduction zone.'"

We laugh, stop, then laugh again.

I want to drive down the dirt road. I can almost kid myself into thinking it would be okay. "Let's check it out," I'd say. Perhaps some of what we have building up inside us could get out before it does any damage. I doubt if we'd get caught.

But I don't know where the road goes. I've lived here for nearly twenty years, and I can't ever recall having been down it before, and I can't see beyond the trees or around the curve. Vick might be frightened or upset.

"Seduction zone," I say, and Vick nods as we pass.

At the quarry, I ask if she wants to walk around, and she shrugs, "Not today."

I toss a pebble in the water. A fish, maybe a turtle, chases the trail of bubbles. We talk about things that don't matter like the weather and the new books at the library and my class schedule that fall. Then she says it's time and pulls off her shirt, kicks off her shorts, dives, disappears under the water, and I try to see where she is, anticipate where she will reappear. There's a ripple and a flash of red, then gone.

I watch, sit on the rock and wave to her when she gets to the far side. She motions for me to jump in, come over beside her, so I pull off my shoes and shirt, wishing I had a flatter stomach, more muscles on my chest.

We swim and splash, half hour, maybe more, then we stop, sit on the rocks, let the sun dry us out, warm us up.

Vick says, "Walt?"

Truck tires crunch on the gravel drive, and Ace waves to us, asks Vick when she's leaving for school. Ace and Vick call back and forth across the pond, then he drops the tailgate, carries a box of tools to his almost finished scuba shop. He glances back at us two, three times.

"I guess we better be going," I say.

But neither of us moves.

We toss small stones in the water. A dozen, fifty, a hundred, more. Some of them are the size of quarters, others not much larger than a grain of sand. Small waves race across the surface then disappear. Vick shivers although the air is warm, and she says she isn't cold. Ace's drill whines in the distance. We throw more rocks. Some land halfway across the pond, others just beyond our feet. It's late, almost dark, and we should be going, heading back, but we keep tossing pebbles, taking turns, moving closer and closer to an unmarked spot somewhere on the surface.

William

(a.k.a. "Highway")

Lubing: Sex and Symbolism
Beneath an '88 Buick

Alfred has a diploma, an '88 Buick and Jenny. The Buick leaks oil, drips puddles everywhere Alf parks. He pulls it into the Lube Shop where we work, pulls it in when things are slow and Ackermann isn't around to yell at us, and we stand down in the bay, look up, wait for the drips to drop. None do. It's like the drips know. Ackermann warned us that the oil was dissolving his parking lot and we were going to be held responsible. He also warned us about calling customers "Dude" and told me I would have been fired already except for what he calls a tight job market. But Alf and I don't listen much to Ackermann and the first week of summer is pretty slow, so we're drip watching when in pulls a red Z-3 Roadster with dual exhausts, the top down, a woman driver and a sorry ass bloodhound's hairy butt planted on the passenger side leather seat. I tell Alf a rich dudette waits, and we argue down in the bay, below the rusted-out Buick, which one of us is going to deal with her because the rich give you a time about doing this and doing that like you are making five hundred dollars an hour, and I lose because Alfred gets shooting pains in his broken arm and swears if I take this one he'll make it up to me big time when the cast comes off.

The woman pushes her sunglasses up on her head, and I ask if she's familiar with our ten-point inspection plan, and she interrupts when I'm getting to the part about free refills on the wiper fluid and says she wants to speak with the young man who talks with dogs. "I'd like for him to speak with Galatea," she says. I don't know what she's going on about and figure she's got the wrong Lube Shop, but then I say, "Galatea?" and she nods at the dog, says it was named after a character in mythology, says it like I wouldn't know because I'm stuck working at this lube place. So, to be cool and because my pimples are gone I say, "Where's Pygmalion?" And she smiles the way pretty rich women can, smiles because she's been caught treating me like a dumb-ass kid, which I used to be.

An old Mercedes, a car as beat up as Alf's Buick, pulls up and I motion for it to go in the other side. Alf gives me a puzzled look, trying to figure out what the rich lady wants, and I signal that I have everything under control, and he smiles relief back and goes to work on the German dream machine.

"Gone," she says without explaining, and then she asks if I'm that young man who communicates with animals.

"Maybe," I answer, although I still have no clue as to who or what she is talking about.

She smiles again and I think of how if she was dressed like a slob I might not give her a second glance, but she's wearing real nice clothes, loose and blousy, and she has this free airy look sitting behind the wheel of this fat ride, and she's got white straight teeth she no doubt bought at the orthodontist, and she smells good, real good, so I give her a second glance although I know she's too old to be the girl in the blue bikini I'm some day soon going to meet.

"You really know how they feel?"

I sigh, give her my look. "Yeah, I know."

She nods like she's digesting all this for some book she's writing or so she can tell her country club friends, but I don't care because she's not bad to look at and smell, and I've moved around the car so I can see her legs, which are tan and streamlined, and I'm getting urges about this older rich lady, which I would not have believed except for my long history of not having sex—I'm mostly virgin on account of not having a car, although I've done it in my dreams ten thousand times at least.

"Just dogs?" she asks.

"Just dogs?" I repeat.

"Can you do this with other animals?"

"Sure," I answer.

"Horses?"

I nod.

"I have a jumper," she says.

"Ok," I say, and I feel a little goofy saying it, like we just agreed to have sex in the back of some horse trailer, "but I don't whisper to 'em."

She laughs and I catch a glimpse of her bra, which wouldn't

ordinarily turn me on, a plain white bra, but my imagination is in overdrive, I think from the caffeine drinking I do hyperventilating my hormone system.

"So, can you tell me what Galatea thinks today?"

"Feels," I say, and I lean over the door, pat the dog, and the dog breathes heavy in my face, which is no boat of gravy, that's for sure.

"How do you do it?" the woman wants to know, and she starts telling me about an old woman who lived in Fairport Harbor—a town five miles down the road where pretty Lake Erie College girls sun themselves on the sandy beach—an old woman who could see these different color lights around a person, an aura, and do I pick up some feeling from the dog, or do I see lights, or do I just look at their posture and expression and sort of interpret things from there.

I give the lady a confused look and then touch my finger to my lips for her to be quiet while the slobbering dog and I press heads. I glance out the corner of my eye at the lady's legs, which are probably one thing she didn't buy because they look pretty authentic and original, and for a second I see us in bed together, her streamlined legs angled this way and that, and lots of dogs sitting on the floor howling their approval. Still, I play it cool, don't run my hands over the leather seats or the rich lady's thighs. "She fixed?" I ask.

The woman shakes her head, says she's just seven months old.

"She's thinking about sex. Powerful urges, almost painful. She really wants to . . . ," I say, and I can tell the woman is worried that I'm going to start naming body parts and saying things like *screw* or *hump*.

She, the woman, not the dog, changes the subject, says thanks, and she hopes that she didn't take too much of my time. She says her name is Anne with an "E", and I say that my name is William with two "L's" but my friends call me Highway with two "H's".

"Highway," she says and she hands me a ten dollar bill. "For your time and help."

I hold up my hand as if I'm not going to take the money but she insists. "A business deal," she calls it. Then she drops her sunglasses back down on her nose and speeds down the street, blond hair and dog ears flapping in the breeze. Alfred pokes his head out from under the Mercedes. "Highway?" he says.

But I don't answer.

A week goes by, nothing much happening except for Alfred's

cast getting nicked up and raunchy. Mornings I spend in the hot rooms of summer school where some moron forgot to put in an air conditioner and the windows open an inch at most. And Lips! Miss Oakley and her plastic water bottle. How could I not watch when she takes a sip. Her hand reaches for the bottle and my pencil stops moving while I wait, watch for the pucker, the drop of water on her bottom lip, her tongue sneaking out to lick it off. Every day she has us write about our life experiences—details, details, she says—while she sits at her desk, reads paperbacks, crosses her legs, dangles a sandal from her toes. It's her first year teaching and she's just learning, but we all think she's going to be good someday.

Afternoons, Alfred and I crawl beneath his car and tighten this and that while I watch and wait for a long-legged girl smelling of suntan lotion and sand to show up and ask where have I been.

Alf calls me pathetic.

Alfred and Jenny—she wears those little tops that scoop way down in the front and show plenty of herself when she leans forward (it would take a much stronger willed person than me not to look)— have shack-up sex at Motel 8 out at Cedar Point on the weekend, which Alf tells me about on Monday morning while we tinker below his Buick, a brown bomb drinking two quarts of oil a week. He grunts and groans while squeezing grease into the fittings—"juice joints," he calls them. "Oh baby, baby, baby," he says. He wiggles and rocks his hips, rolls his eyes, "It feels so good."

I'm tempted to write about Alfred's experiences in my essays except for Miss Oakley saying we should write about ourselves and avoid writing sex, which for me has been easy to do.

Alf and I don't see the woman or dog for two weeks, and I'm thinking that's the last of her I'll ever see or smell when she shows up in her BMW with the formerly horny Galatea slobbering on the seat.

I look up and can pretty much figure out what's coming, but I don't beat a path to her car. I don't want to give the idea that I need to play Doctor Laura for screwed up dogs. Still, she smiles real big so I saunter over, wiping my hands on a rag as I go.

"Highway," she says when I get to her door, and for a second I don't even know what she's talking about.

"Anne," I answer.

"You're not going to believe this," she says. "Galatea came into heat the day after we were here. You were right." She grins a little at saying "heat" and acts surprised and excited at the same time.

She stares at me for a long time, so me not being stupid, I'm wondering what does a forty-year-old rich lady with perfect legs and teeth and who probably drops a hundred bucks a week on her hair want with an eighteen-year-old guy who makes six-fifty an hour at the Lube Shop, doesn't have a car and won't graduate even until the end of summer school.

"Horses," she says. "You said you could do this with horses?"

Alfred has joined us—probably so he could check out her legs, which I told him about—and I introduce him and her, and Alfred says, "Of course he can do horses."

Anne draws a little map on the back of a discount Lube card and asks if I would come out tomorrow evening and—"what do you really call it?"—with her jumper horse, Doc.

"Communicate," says Alf.

Alfred gives me a time afterwards, saying that she is hot to trot for my body, but I'm not that stupid even if I was kicked out of school a few weeks early.

I tell Alf to leave me alone. The oil is dripping that hot ugly smell, and he stops and stares at me. "You're a virgin, aren't you? Aren't you?"

I don't like the way he's grinning and I say, "No!" and he says, "Who, who?" like he's an owl.

I tell him I don't talk about it afterwards and that doing it is not some mechanical thing like lubricating a universal joint and he should know because he has Jenny.

He just stands there and laughs while the oil drips and the jerk sitting in the car above us wants to know what the hell is going on.

All day while we're working on the cars, Alfred will stop and look at me and whisper. "A virgin, a kicked out of school virgin." He warns me that we're at our sexual peak, and if I do not release my desires—"wants," he calls them—hormones will overwhelm my body and damage my mind, that my privates will shrivel and shrink, become wrinkled and useless.

"What happened to Chuck Doll's 'Vette when he redlined the engine and never popped the clutch?" he asks.

"He blew the engine," I answer.

Alf nods. "I rest my case."

I know that Alf is giving me a tough time and making it all up, practicing for the day he will become a lawyer, but I can't sleep at night for thinking about the engine on Chuck's '66 'Vette and wondering.

Next day in English I write a paper about my animal communicating and get a B minus and would have had an A except for Miss Oakley saying that my comments about squirting grease into the cars was off the topic and that I needed more details. Details, details, she says.

On the way out of class I drop a free lube coupon on her desk and hope it will help me get an A on the next paper.

Alf and I head out in his Buick to Waite Hill, which is where Art Modell who stole the Cleveland Browns to Baltimore once lived, and we get to Anne's bigger-than-the-Holiday-Inn house. Her husband isn't around, which is ok by me, but Galatea comes running out to greet us and then Anne and then her daughter, who looks like she's my age almost. Her having a daughter standing there popping gum and eyeing me like I'm some fly that flew off the manure pile pretty much kills my thoughts of sex with her mother. We all walk out to the barn looking pretty much like a friggin parade.

Doc the horse is wound tighter than cheap string on a plastic yo-yo, prancing and dancing so much that I don't even go near him. Anne's daughter lurks around for a few seconds, gives a deep sigh like she's bored and goes back to the house to play Nintendo or hum along with the radio or who knows what. Then a horn honks and Anne smiles, says her daughter has a date, another example of the power you have when you've got a ride.

I'm getting ready to make something up about Doc when he calms down and begins to sniff, check me out. We're in the barn, me and Anne and Alfred. Anne's in riding boots, which some men like—I could be one—and pants so tight you could read the date on a dime in her pocket, but I'm not having any sex thoughts even though her daughter is gone. It worries me, like I might have hurt myself or maybe damaged the goods from holding back like Alf swore would happen. I look at the hay and try to imagine Anne and me tossing about in it. I think about her smooth legs. I glance at those riding boots, but I don't get any urges. None! The horse comes over and sniffs my hair, then it looks down at me with the huge brown eyes and we smash heads pretty hard.

"Worried," I say.

"Worried?" Anne asks.

I nod.

"Worried," Her tone a mixture of disbelief and excitement. "Yes, oh my. Yes, that's possible. Of course."

But she doesn't explain a thing, and I rub the horse's nose for a second and it jerks away, probably from the smell of grease, which is impossible to get off my hands. "Gotta go," I say, and then Alf and I hurry home because it's almost nine o'clock, and I have this probation curfew thing hanging around my neck.

A few days later, Anne stops and asks me to come out and see Doc her jumper horse again. "I think I've got things taken care of," she says, then winks.

Alfred hears what she says and sees the wink and later when we're tightening nuts on his '88 Buick, which is guzzling oil faster than gasoline, he sings "Hot to trot," like he was a moron.

After work I take his car, but Alf doesn't go because he has other plans, like getting his cast off, something I was hoping to take care of for him. When I get to Anne's, the two of us go to the barn and there's no sign of the daughter or husband or even Galatea for that matter. I'm standing there pretending to study Doc while smelling Anne's shampooed hair and listening to her whisper about this and that, which I don't really follow because of the distraction her half-unbuttoned blouse is to my concentration. I'm sneaking peeks and out of nowhere she says: "Do me."

I see part of her breast swelling up over the top of her bra, the only older woman's breast I have ever seen in person although it may not count yet because I haven't seen all of it, only the upper third, but it's a good third, and I hear her saying something, but the words don't sink in, they don't register.

"Do me," she says again.

I stop breathing.

"Do you?" I ask.

She nods, steps close, as close as she can step without going through me. "Now," she says, and then she leans forward, our hip bones bumping, other places touching, and she puts her head against mine, and I get the want signals loud and clear.

Her eyes are wide open, looking, waiting, her breath warm on my chin, and I stand there not moving because I'm in some kind of state. Her urges zap me in the brain like I have headphones in my ears and some song is going full blast, exploding inside my head singing, "Do me, do me, do me."

I run.

I fly around the corner of the barn like my pants are on fire, which they almost are, nearly slipping on the grass and killing myself, but I get to the Buick and jump in and pray that it'll start, and I spin the tires on the red brick drive, and the car jumps maybe twenty feet and stalls. I glance back to see if she's coming, and I see a black puddle of oil in the middle of the drive that has leaked out of Alfred's piece of crap car and is going to be hell for someone to clean up. I get the car started again and shoot out of there like I'm running first at Daytona.

I bounce and weave down the road as fast as Alf's Buick will take me. The red engine warning light flashes on and telephone poles zip by as fast as a picket fence. I get away without any speeding tickets, which is a miracle, and I'm heading back on Route 90, part of me relieved to be safe and parts of me feeling real disappointed.

The next day, in English class, I write about how Anne kept coming back to the Lube Shop because she had this horse and how Alfred put the hot to trot song in my mind. I write about how we were pressing heads, and she was saying, "Do me," and I really had the urge in my loins and in my fingertips but how I had the run signal in my feet. I describe the oil spot Alfred's car left there in the drive and that it might have been symbolic if Anne and I had done something, but we didn't so it was just a spot. I write about the red warning light blinking in the car and how that might have meant something, too, like hold my horses, maybe Anne hadn't been thinking sex at all.

Later, Alf gives me a hard time beneath the Buick and says that I have some serious problems. But I say Anne might have an NRA type husband who could have shown up with a gun or she might have gotten pregnant, had a little Highway and I would be paying support for some rich kid who would probably go to Harvard.

Alf says that I have probably already done irreversible damage to my brain and body parts from the way I have stifled my urges. He thinks the same thing must have happened to his Buick and just look at it.

A drop of oil falls between us.

"No more animal communicating," I say. "No more."

For two weeks I grease cars, change the oil and fill the windshield wiper reservoirs with fluid. I pump tires full of air, install new air filters and PC valves. I finish summer school, spend evenings flying kites at the beach. I don't call customers dude. I don't communicate.

Alf gets a '93 Ford pickup, which he has named the love wagon, and he and Jenny take it to the drive-in and park in the back row. The truck owns more than a hundred thousand miles but it doesn't leak, and Alf says it saves them a bundle over nights at Motel 8. Alf sells me his Buick for fifty bucks and the understanding that I will take care of any potential problem customers.

So, when an old Mustang pulls in with a rumbling exhaust, something we do not fix, Alf nods that this car is mine.

It's Miss Oakley and a dog with a huge head, a bear head.

"William," she says.

"Miss Oakley," I answer. I wipe my hands on a rag and tell her that we do not replace mufflers. Then I ask if she knows about our ten-point inspection plan.

"I stopped because of Henry," she says.

I nod at Henry. Henry nods back.

"I was wondering," she says. "A big favor? In your essay you said you could . . . would you . . . do you mind . . . with Henry?"

Behind me, Alf is whistling one of his made up songs.

I step closer to the car. Miss Oakley rubs bear dog's head, takes a sip of water from her plastic bottle. The strap of a blue bra, maybe a bathing suit, slips off her shoulder. She pushes it back, glances at me, then rubs Henry's head one more time.

"Sure," I say. "Sure."

Chautauqua

Kurt's my friend. He loves his wife, his dog, his house, his car. He'd love his kids, too, if he had any. He drinks little, swears less, shakes hands with a strong grip and crosses his legs when he sits. He can whistle through his teeth, but I've never seen him spit.

Kurt meditates, runs, lifts weights, does forty laps every morning in the Heisley club pool. He eats tofu, yogurt, fiber and sprouts, avoids red meat because of the killer he claims it is.

Kurt and Kathy have been married four years. Four! And I was at the wedding. It was something.

I'm in bed and the phone rings. I pick it up and say: "Hey, Kurt," before he says a word. I know it's him, his ring.

"Come up tomorrow," he says.

Kurt and Kathy are spending weekends at Chautauqua. He's rented a small place there for the summer. Kurt says that if a man neglects his artistic nature, his feminine side, he becomes one-dimensional. Kurt studies painting, listens to the orchestra, attends lectures, gets cultured, rides his bike and golfs. Kathy swims, sits on the beach.

Shortly after Kurt and Kathy got married, Kurt inherited tons of money. "It has changed my life," he says.

"Tomorrow?" I ask.

"Tomorrow," Kurt says.

I say, "For sure," although I know I shouldn't, that I have other things I need to do. But I figure we'll ride bikes, maybe swim, too, and, besides, what are friends for. I sell kites and bikes, have a little store in Fairport Harbor down near the beach, the prettiest beach in all Ohio. East of us we have the nuke plant cooling towers, to the west we have Cleveland. Everyone comes to our beach. I sell kites that do loops and dives, big kites, too, big enough to lift a kid off the ground, but my favorites are the old box kites. You can get them up there high enough to hang on a cloud. Nothing like biking either. Wind and wheels, legs and lungs. I keep my bike in the bedroom, hang it from hooks in the ceiling. "Want to bike?" I ask. "Swim? I'll bring a couple kites."

"Golf," Kurt says.

I say sure, I'll be there.

Kurt hangs up happy, rolls against Kathy and goes to sleep. I stare at the ceiling, Frances at my feet. I hate golf.

I might get my own dog. Frances is a Lab with papers and a family tree, a five hundred dollar dog. Kurt's dog. Smart as some people I know. Smarter. And she has a soft mouth. Kurt bought Frances when he was duck hunting in the Dakotas. She was a pup, fit in the pocket of his winter coat, but she now weighs sixty-five pounds, sleeps next to me on the weekends, dreams and makes little woofing noises.

Kurt's too good. It isn't healthy. You need vices to let go of when you get a problem, like a tail on a kite, things you can drop when the breeze gets light and you find yourself falling.

Kathy isn't like Kurt. Kurt's dark (in the winter, artificially tanned); Kathy's fair, a Finn. Finns are survivors, live next door to the Ruskies, there on the Arctic Circle. They steam themselves in saunas, then jump into lakes of ice water. Guts, determination and stubbornness: *Sisu*. Kathy taught me that. Kathy teaches seventh graders in some poor school in Cleveland. Kathy: Blond, blue-eyed *sisu*. *Sisu* with a dimple. She makes me laugh. She's a card, that's what people say: "Kathy, she's a card."

Legs. I love legs. I could stare at them for hours. I don't gawk, but how can you not notice. Kurt can do it, not notice, a man with an iron will. I'm weak.

Kurt calls two, three times a week, says meet me after work and we'll go for a ride over into Pennsylvania, over to the quarries. He wants to ride his bike around the Great Lakes. He has given up hunting and is now searching for ways to get closer to nature. "To become one again with our original mother," he says.

Sometimes, Kurt forgets he called, that he asked me to come over, and he doesn't come straight home. He might be swimming laps or lifting weights. Kathy and I sit on the front porch steps, wait and talk. Once, I stood up and brushed off the seat of my shorts, and she said, "Know your problem, Highway?"

I said, "No," and she said, "You have no ass."

Kathy and I fell in the grass laughing. You can't get Kurt to say, "darn," and there's Kathy telling me I have no ass. But she's right. I have skinny tendencies, which is one of the reasons it's difficult getting a date. A few bad habits and a slight stammer don't help either. I have worn a sweatshirt under a shirt, pushed it up in the arms to make it look like muscles. Kurt has muscles like the biker, golfer, runner, he is.

One time Kathy met me at the door, shook her head and pointed upstairs. "The bathroom," she said.

"I haven't got the urge," I answered and she said, "No, go on up. It's Kurt. You've got to see this." She shook her head again.

I climbed the steps. "Kurt," I said. "Kurt."

"In here," he said, his voice coming from behind the closed door.

"I'll wait downstairs," I said. I moved away from the door, which he then pushed open. Kurt's foot was in the sink, lather on his leg. He was dabbing a spot he'd nicked.

"What's up?" I asked.

He ran the razor down his shin bone, then under the faucet. "It'll be easier to pick out the gravel if there's a crash, less wind resistance, too," he said.

I sat on the pot and watched.

"We're going to do it, aren't we?" he asked, looking at me in the mirror. "Around the lakes."

A drop of blood fell into the sink. "Sure," I said. "Sure."

Kurt finished his legs and toweled them dry, splashed on aftershave, rubbed his hand up and down the smooth, shiny skin.

Kathy squeezed my arm when I came down the steps. She squeezed through the long-sleeved sweatshirt and into my skinny arms until I could feel the tip of her fingernails digging into my skin. "It's okay," I whispered, "your legs are still much prettier than his." Her fingers squeezed my arm one more time. When Kurt and I were on the bikes, I glanced back, and she was looking at his legs and making this funny face.

I ride hairy-legged.

Saturday morning I pack the bikes and kite in the truck. Kurt says Chautauqua is no place for a dog, so I press my head against Frances, that soft spot on top between the ears. Frances wishes she could go along but she understands too.

I know dogs.

Chautauqua's two hours away, a town and a lake in New York State, and the lake's big, maybe five, six miles long. Maybe more. The town's small, isn't really a town—they call it an institute, honest to God, an institute—and it has a wall around it. A wall! I park the truck across the street, the only truck in the lot. Two bucks. I walk up to the gates, whistling and filling my mind with pure thoughts. It's that kind of place. The smart-looking man at the ticket counter says, seven bucks. I say, "Damn," and the good, intelligent people in line give me arched-eyebrow, pursed-lip looks to let me know dirty talk is not acceptable here.

Inside, people shuffle around like they're in a library or at a funeral, talk in low voices and are in no hurry to go anywhere. They sit on front porches behind boxes of flowers or on the park bench reading a newspaper or a hardback book. Lectures, operas, ballet, concerts, old people, ministers, retired school teachers. Everybody smart and peaceful. If I were to visit on a regular basis, I'd need a haircut and wire rimmed-glasses.

I find Kathy and she does a little skip and sticks out her arm like I'm to escort her around. She's a card. There's a dimple high on her cheekbone, just a little below her eye, not a wrinkle, a tiny dent. Kurt's out wind surfing on the lake. He bumped into someone, she says. Kathy and I stroll in a big circle, go around the amphitheater, the bookstore, and the Tally Ho Hotel. We take our time, in no hurry to get anywhere. We stop at the Sweet Art Shop and get cones, then sit on the library steps. Kathy says Sinful Chocolate is the best, holds it in front of my face. I take a lick and say, yes, yes indeed.

Kathy says Kurt will be back before lunch.

I nod and say no hurry. An hour here and the place is growing on me.

Kathy and I browse the bookstore. She's got this favorite author, Rick Bass. Here, here, she says pulling on my elbow, listen to this. She reads to me, whispering between the aisles. Do you like it? she asks.

I nod, say, I do.

We buy the book to read in the park while we wait for Kurt, but we no sooner find a bench and up he pops.

He flashes in the Chautauqua sun: silver sunglasses, large white teeth, gold chain around his neck, an Irish pinkie ring, smooth shaved legs and slicked back hair. Kathy and I hold up our hands to shield our eyes.

We golf. Me and Kurt. How I hate the game. Mindless. Walk, walk, walk, whisper, whack, whisper, walk, walk, walk. I won't go except to drink beer and swear and get on Kurt's nerves. The clothes! The hats! And you can't take off your shirt. Not allowed.

But Kurt's good. Patience, control, concentration. He could write a book. He's got it all: leather bag, parrot-green slacks, the white shoes with the fringed flaps.

Some jerk behind us laughs and makes nasty remarks when I swing at the ball, and Kurt keeps saying, "Don't worry about it." Every time I swing, we can hear the jerk chuckle seventy, eighty yards behind us. I line up, swing. Whack. The ball dribbles down the fairway. Jerk slaps his thigh. "Heh, heh, heh."

Kurt goes, "Don't worry about it."

I wave my club at the pale jerk, but his soapy thick forehead doesn't get the hint, so I take out my shag balls, balls I found in the woods or lifted off the course. I tee them up, seven of them, take out my number three driver and let fly, aiming for the bright spot above his eyes. The first two fly wide on account of my bad slice, but after that I begin to adjust. He dives behind his cart, although none come that close. Maybe one.

But nothing disturbs Kurt. The concentration! He steps up to the ball, and I hold my breath, make no rude noises. Kurt lines it up and thwack. It hooks off the end of his club, heads for the trees. Leaves and small limbs fall to the ground. Kurt stands there, shakes his head and says, "No."

"No?" I say. "Damn it, Kurt. Can't you say *shit* or throw your club or something? What's wrong with you?"

I pick up my golfball, let out a Tarzan yell, throw it as far as I can, farther than I usually hit them, then dump my bag upside down and kick the clubs, tees and the two beer cans that fall out. "Do I have to do it for you, Kurt?" I ask.

I rip the putter out of my bag and throw it toward the trees. It whirls through the air like a loose helicopter blade, then I tee up one of the beer cans and hit it with a nine iron. Foam everywhere.

We meet Kathy back at the Institute. Kathy stands on the porch, sniffs the geraniums potted there, goes "hmmm." Kurt says if we hurry we can catch the lecture. I ask Kathy if she is going to come. She rolls her eyes, shakes her head.

The lecture hall is packed. "The Disappearance of the Small Town Newspaper." YAWN. After half an hour, the man, who is a reporter with, I think, the *Times*, is still talking about what happened to newspapers in the Thirties, and all these people are sitting there nodding, sitting on the edge of their seats. It gives me goose bumps, I swear.

Afterward, Kurt and I walk to the beach, pass through a replica of the Holy Land on the way. The Dead Sea, Bethlehem, Jerusalem, Galilee, all there at our feet. Amazing stuff and I feel guilty that I don't know more about all this and that I am full of impure thoughts.

We find a bench; Kurt sits on one end, me on the other. We sit and watch the sailboats on the lake.

First thing I think of when I see a lake like this is that I want to swim across. It would be touch and go, that's how big it is, but I'm close to doing it, ripping off my clothes and diving in.

Two women pass, give Kurt the double take. One is in jeans, but the other is wearing those nylon running shorts, bright red with a slit up the side. A runner: spring in her step, small ankles, thin legs but muscle, too, enough. I glance at Kurt but he's not looking. I don't fall off the bench or lean forward. I'm not obvious. Only my eyeballs move, slowly rotate inside my head.

So I'm sitting here at Chautauqua, the Holy Land behind me, sailboats in front, long, bare legs swinging by, and Kurt says he's coming here every weekend. Every weekend. Golf. Sail. Learn the arts.

I say, Kurt, get a life, yell, raise hell, go somewhere, do something, look at legs.

I do love legs. Spring and summer. Sweet heaven. Bring back the miniskirts.

Kurt ain't like that. I don't think he ever looks. We were at a basketball game. Cavs versus Chicago. Go Cavs, but you got to love the Bulls, too. Three women sit next to us, next to Kurt. The one beside Kurt hikes up a skirt and crosses her black nylon legs and my eyes almost fall into the popcorn. I don't say a thing. Kurt looks at me, slowly shakes his head, says, "Highway, you're terrible."

I watch the woman in the red running shorts disappear beyond the Sea of Galilee. Kurt is staring out at the lake, but he shakes his head and says, "Highway, Highway, Highway."

Kurt is like a roadblock, a warning sign, flashing red lights on my secret thoughts.

He leans forward on the bench. His elbows rest on his knees. His fingers are laced together as if in prayer, a cat thinking pure thoughts.

Kurt loves Chautauqua: the peace, the arts, the culture, the time to reflect. He wants to be an artist of the oil painting type. He wants to do it all and he will.

Kathy makes me laugh, that little skip she does.

Kurt doesn't look at me when we talk. He stares out at the water or the cottages on the far side. It's like we're two spies sitting in Red Square. I want to call him Comrade Kurt. He gets up, stretches, and we walk back towards the place he rents on one of the little brick streets. We pass flower boxes full of petunias and red geraniums. I wrinkle my forehead, pretend to ponder.

Kurt and Kathy say, stay over, don't go back, don't be silly. But I'm not sure. Chautauqua has a wall around it, the bike is still in the truck, and Frances is alone at home.

Kurt says stay awhile, at least until he gets back from his art class. I call Kurt a Renaissance man, and he laughs real hard and shakes his head, then says, "You think?" And I say, "Hell, yes," like I usually do and he smiles, so I say it one more time. "A Renaissance man." Kurt's smile grows until I see his molars.

Kathy says she wants to swim, and it's a warm day, so I agree to stay a little longer. Kurt runs to art class; Kathy and I go to the beach.

We swim, get rowdy, splash and yank each other's legs out from under. She stands on her head in the water, only legs and feet sticking above the surface. Long toes, red toenails. And the young kids are watching us and smiling like aren't we the strange ones. Kathy and I swim to the ropes, and then, just to annoy the lifeguard and because she is Finn, we duck under and swim beyond. We talk back and forth over the top of the water, pretend we're the only ones on the whole lake, maybe the only ones in the whole world.

The lifeguard, an old man, is standing on his chair, blowing his whistle as if we're going to drown, and he's thinking no one's gone beyond the ropes since Jimmy Carter grew peanuts and that he's sure going to have a lot to tell his friends. Kathy and I turn, swim towards the beach, which is not sand at all but grass and flowers. This is, after all, Chautauqua.

We get out, sit on a towel. Kathy watches the sailboats out on the lake. She points with a long finger at a butterfly, pretty and perfect, in the daisies, going from one flower to another, drinking the juices. Bubbles of water evaporate from her shoulders and legs and her dark blue bikini.

By the time Kurt arrives, Kathy and I are dry and in the middle of discussing which of the distant houses we would most like for our own. Kurt shows us a stack of prints he's been studying. Gosh, he says, there's so much to learn. But he loves it and is going back to the studio after supper. He shows us his camel hair brushes and explains the proper way to arrange the paints on the palette. He talks about art and creativity and the total being greater than the sum of the parts. He hasn't started painting yet, but he knows a lot about washing the canvas to make it warm or cool, and he's got ideas.

We walk through the Holy Land, through Galilee, Judea and Samaria, back to the quiet house on the quiet street. Kurt and Kathy and me. I tell them I'm going home, back to Frances and Ohio.

No, no, they both say. No. Please stay.

I shake my head. I don't think it's a good idea, my staying any longer.

Kathy grabs my arm and says, if I leave her alone in this place, she'll never forgive me. I say I'll think about it, that I'd like to stay, but I don't want to crowd them and how about Frances. She's at my place and I'm watching her for them, and I hate to leave her alone like that.

Kurt smacks his forehead, says he is not going duck hunting anymore, a violation of nature, he says. Kurt offers to sell me Frances, then he says, no, she's mine if I want her. I look at Kathy and she looks at me and we all take turns looking at each other. She's a good dog, he says.

I laugh and Kurt says to think about it.

After supper, Kurt's eager to get to his studio and learn artistic things, and, if it goes well, he'll have something to show us when he gets back. I'm still undecided. It isn't good for a dog to be neglected. I call my sister and ask if she'll check on Frances, and she says, of course.

Kurt keeps looking at his watch, and I think maybe he's changed his mind and wants me to go, but when I mention going, he says, no, that we'll run in the morning, maybe a fast bike ride around the lake.

He excuses himself, says he is eager to get started. Kathy and I make jokes about that's how those artists are.

From the window, I watch Kurt run down the street in the direction of where the art building might be. Kathy and I move to the front porch. I sit in a chair with my size twelve's on the railing, rock back and forth on the hind legs and twiddle my thumbs. Old folks walk by and we exchange nods, me fooling them on who and what I am. Kathy swings back and forth in the porch swing, her bare feet skimming the floor each time she comes forward. It looks funny, me rocking in the chair and her rocking alone in the swing, so I go sit beside her, and the old couples walking by give us bigger grins than before. I grin back.

Hours pass. The sun goes down, the air gets cool. I see stars between the leaves of the trees. A light breeze, perfect for a small kite, carries the smell of nearby suppers. From time to time, we hear water splash at the lake and dishes being stacked in a neighbor's sink. The orchestra is playing. I can hear violins and drums and the chains on the swing going creak, creak, creak. Kathy and I talk in soft voices, her whispers warm on my face.

Marlene

Charades

The car, a '66 Mercedes, owns two hundred and fifty thousand miles and a bad muffler, but it's plowing through the snow. The man, Larry, calls the car a tank, says it with affection, patting the dash, then caressing the steering wheel. "The tank will get us through," he says. The woman, Marlene, grim-faced and cold, is looking out her window at the mailboxes that have been knocked off their posts by a snowplow that passed over these roads earlier.

Marlene, is pretty—Larry's father once told Larry that she had Julie Christie lips—but she's hunkered down inside her coat, staring out her window, not feeling pretty at all.

Larry glances at her from time to time while trying to keep his eyes on the road. Larry's eyes: twenty/twenty, dark brown, warm and gentle. Only twenty-five and already trimmed with grinkles—that's what Marlene calls them—grin wrinkles around his eyes. That was one of the things Marlene loved about him when she met him her first year out of college.

Marlene is angry. Hurt. Jealous. She doesn't know how she feels exactly. She doesn't know if it's okay to feel these things. Upset. That would be a good place to start. Upset. She would like for Larry to reach out and touch her, tell her she's pretty—she's never seen a Julie Christie movie and could not, therefore, appreciate the compliment about her lips.

She's been worried for some time that something's wrong, that Larry no longer loves her the way he once did, that their marriage might be falling apart like all those other marriages she reads about in her magazines. No one is happy anymore. Not for long. Thinking this makes her even more unhappy, but she doesn't know how to stop. She has a tendency to over-analyze things—"analysis paralysis," Larry calls it—but still, she can't shake the feeling that things aren't right, are not the way she wants them to be. They're sliding down a hill—not the car, although from time to time it slips a little too. Their relationship.

Her confusion, anger and hurt are made worse by the coziness of the car moving through the snow and the Christmas lights twinkling on the houses they pass. She's tempted to open the door and leap. If she landed in a snow bank, she'd probably be okay. She wraps her fingers around the handle.

The clouds and moon are fighting too. Marlene sees symbolism and omens lurking in almost everything and would be interested in the conflict taking place in the sky if she were a casual observer, someone sitting in the backseat watching the couple in front, but she's too upset, too involved in her own turmoil.

She presses herself against the seat. One minute snow is falling, swirling in the headlights, and the next, the clouds move aside and the air is clear, there are shadows, a few stars.

Larry leans forward, "It's like millions of diamonds," he says.

The farms out here in this area southeast of Cleveland are mostly Amish and the houses are undecorated, quiet and dark and somehow look even more Christmas-like than the decorated homes in Unity. Still, she doesn't understand why their friend Kenneth chooses to live so far out from town.

"It's like millions of diamonds," Larry repeats. He points at the snow swirling in the beam of the headlights.

Marlene looks at the snow, then thinks of the not large, not perfect diamond on her finger. Larry gave her the ring while they were at his apartment watching the ball fall in Times Square. (Larry often jokes that he proposed one year and she said yes the next.) A few weeks later, they were in a jewelry store, and he insisted that she look at the ring under the Gemscope. "The flaw's tiny," he said.

Flaw talk bothered her. "It doesn't matter," she said, thinking it would be perfect if she wasn't forced to look.

Larry insisted. He said something about being honest and repeated that the flaw was tiny, it almost didn't exist.

At first, she hadn't been able to see the small inclusion for all the brilliance around it. Only after Larry coaxed her into looking a second time did she see it. A dark spot.

Marlene's secret fear is that there's never going to be enough time, that she'll never live long enough. Marlene wants to live with intensity, squeeze all the passion and love out of every minute. When she was a girl she admired President Kennedy, the way he seemed to get the most out of every day. And Jackie too. Marlene teaches French, maybe that's the connection. Weren't Jackie's ancestors French? The French have passion and she likes to think she does too.

She and Larry have promised each other that they wouldn't be like other couples: arguing about petty things, no longer holding hands, forgetting to kiss good-bye, saying, "luv ya," instead of "I love you," going to bed at different times, fighting, having affairs, getting a divorce. She wants to live and love the way John and Jackie did.

"Sure is a pretty night," Larry mumbles, and Marlene wonders if he's doing this to annoy her. The snow has stopped and a few stars peek between the breaks in the clouds. She's tempted to say, *I heard you the first time*. It is a pretty night, and it irritates her that she can't enjoy it fully and that he can. It makes her feel more alone despite the closeness of the car, and time is racing by. Seconds, minutes, hours, the entire evening. She doesn't know why she thinks like this. Sometimes she wants to reach out and grab it, grab time, and hold it down so she can catch her breath, and she and Larry can solve all their problems and misunderstandings without a second lost.

Marlene stares at the snow and picks at the emotional scab the evening has become. She is convinced that Ken and Sylvia are probably discussing her and Larry at this very moment, saying that there seemed to be a little bit of trouble in paradise.

(Ken and Sylvia are not, in fact, discussing Larry and Marlene. Ken and Sylvia are in bed making love. They did not clean up the dishes or even bother turning out the kitchen light or the blue blinking lights that decorate the front window. Sylvia, who is Russian, is whispering a phrase over and over in Ken's ear, and, although he doesn't know what it means, the words' strange sound and her warm breath adds to the intensity of their lovemaking.)

Earlier in the evening, Sylvia had amused Marlene, the way she spoke English in a sing-song manner, and called Ken, "Ken-Yeth." From time to time she asked, "How do you say that?" and then struggled to explain what it was she wanted to know. Sylvia's movements were fluid and graceful and fun to watch, almost as if she had been an actress or in the ballet in Russia before coming to the States. (She was not—she was a teacher.) Abstractions were the most difficult for her, feelings and emotions. "What is this?" she asked as she frowned and hugged her knees to her chest.

"Lonely," Larry said before anyone else had a chance. Sylvia rolled the word around in her mouth. "Lonely," she said. "I am lonely for my friends, yes?"

Marlene thought that Sylvia wasn't as pretty as Ken's previous girlfriend. She had a high forehead made worse by the way she pulled her hair straight back, and she was tall and bony, not at all the short, plump Russian that Marlene had expected and maybe hoped for, but she made Ken and Larry laugh—Ken had taught her a few swear words—and there had been something feminine about her movements, the way she tapped the back of Ken's hand with her fingernail, the expressive eyes.

Ken and Sylvia had moved around the kitchen like dancers, leaning into each other while they filled glasses and set out plates, his hand brushing her back when she passed, her fingers playfully poking his ribs or sliding down his arm. During dinner, Marlene could see from the angle of Ken's arm that he was resting his hand—not always resting—on Sylvia's leg.

Marlene squeezed Larry's leg and once rested her hand on his arm, but Larry did not return the affection. He talked about the weather: low pressure areas, winter storms, how much snow was expected that night, temperatures in the teens after the front passed. Once, Marlene interrupted Larry's weather talk with: "I know how we can get warm later."

Ken laughed, then squeezed Sylvia on the leg. Maybe Ken was thinking about getting warm later, too, but Larry smiled and went back to a point he was trying to make about how the winters were getting worse than when he was a kid, didn't everyone think so?

Sylvia said that Moscow winters were much worse.

"*Kholahdnah*?" Larry asked.

Sylvia hesitated, smiled, then answered in Russian. Before Marlene could ask what they were saying, Larry responded with an entire string of sounds—sentences, she guessed.

"You speak Russian well," Sylvia said, her eyes opening wide, as if she not only heard the words but could see them.

"*Sposeebo*," he answered, then he added something that made Sylvia laugh.

Marlene knew that Larry had taken Russian in college and assumed that he still knew a few words, but this was far more than she had expected. Larry didn't know a word of French despite her attempts to teach him. She didn't like that he could talk to this woman, make her laugh, and she didn't have a clue as to what he was saying. "What?" Marlene asked.

Larry hesitated, maybe shifting his brain back to English, maybe reluctant to explain.

"Cold?" Larry said. "I asked her if it was cold." He shrugged, then looked at Sylvia. "It's a beautiful language, but I'm afraid I've forgotten most of it."

Sylvia said, "No, Larry, no," drawing out the words, almost singing them, NOOooo LAReeee, NOoo, then launching into Russian again. Marlene heard *parooski* which she thought was the word for Russian, but she didn't recognize anything else.

Larry waved his hands and pointed his fingers while talking, as far as Marlene could tell, as if Russian were his native language. (Marlene, who has a very active imagination, might have wondered, under more favorable conditions, if Larry was actually a Russian spy, checking out the real estate market in America, an exciting possibility if it hadn't been for her being so upset that he was carrying on this conversation with a woman—perhaps she was the spy—a woman who had somehow become more attractive as the evening wore on.)

Marlene decided she didn't like the language, that despite what Larry had said about it being pretty, it wasn't. The swishes, the hisses, the snaps of T's were too . . . too rough.

"Excuse me," Marlene said, as she left them and went to the bathroom.

It was humiliating. Larry didn't have enough sense to know that he looked and sounded silly, that talking when others can't understand you is rude. It was like playing charades, something Marlene absolutely refused to do. Everyone staring at you, no one knowing what you're trying to say.

She looked in the mirror. She had gained six pounds since Thanksgiving and it showed in her face. (Marlene is pregnant although she does not yet know it.)

When Marlene returned to the table, Sylvia was biting her bottom lip, wiping her eyes with the corner of her napkin. Marlene wasn't sure what had moved Sylvia so deeply, whether it was hearing her native language or something Larry had said.

More Russian was spoken. Larry never put his hand on Marline's knee. Ken and Sylvia wrestled, tickled, teased, seemed to be the couple that Larry and Marlene once were.

Larry starts to point at something out Marlene's window when the tires slip on the snow, and the car slides toward the ditch on her side. A wiggle, which he corrects, but Marlene throws herself back in the seat as if preparing for a crash. "Careful," she says.

Larry taps the temperature gauge. "It'll be warm in a minute." He holds the wheel with both hands and shakes his head. "The shadows look blue, don't they?"

Marlene glances out the window, pretends to shiver.

"Sure you're okay?" Larry asks.

"Yes," she answers, clearly not. She is angry with him and would gladly tell him so, but she feels guilty. The warm down coat she is wearing was a Christmas gift, and he was obviously excited about giving it to her. Besides, for Marlene, saying you're angry is like admitting you're at fault.

"Heat," Larry says. He turns the knob up as a high as it will go and within seconds the air pouring out of the vent is burning Marlene's ankles. She wonders if Larry turned the blower up to the highest notch to hurt her.

"Better?" he asks.

She stomps her feet on the floor mat. "They're numb," she says. Marlene looks over her shoulder at the road behind them. There's no one there but she has the feeling of being watched.

Larry is pulling into the apartment driveway when Marlene unfastens her seatbelt. She knows that it irritates him. "You seem impatient," he'd said once before and then, "It really isn't safe, you know."

Marlene jumps from the car as soon as it stops, doesn't wait or look back to see if Larry's coming. She shuffles through the snow, and, by the time Larry is in the doorway stomping the snow from his shoes, she has her coat off and is in the kitchen listening to the phone ring, which she does not answer. (A call from her mother or someone looking for a house. Both mother and buyers call at all hours.)

The phone stops ringing and Larry wrinkles his nose. The apartment smells of something dead, a mouse maybe, maybe mold growing beneath the damp carpet, but they have not been able to find anything. "I feel like you're running away from me when you do that," he says, remaining near the door as if they might do it over again, go back to the car and walk in together.

She wants to ask him if he knows how to say that in Russian, but she doesn't. "I was cold." She is tempted to say it in French, but she knows Larry would laugh and tell her that he loves it when she talks sexy like that.

Larry opens the refrigerator, his coat still on. He lifts out a bowl of Jell-O salad, a bowl they had meant to take to Ken's but had forgotten, and begins to spoon it directly from the bowl to his mouth, something he would never have been comfortable doing when they were dating. It irritates her that he is so happy, that he can shrug off this problem as if it is nothing. It bothers her even more that some of his happiness might have come from talking Russian with Sylvia.

"Sure you're okay?" he asks.

Marlene nods, looks away. Marlene thinks that if you have to ask someone to apologize it doesn't count. Same for asking someone if they love you. If you have to ask, their answer doesn't count.

Larry wants to go for a walk in the snow and asks Marlene to go along, but Marlene says she's going to bed.

Larry follows her into the bedroom—his coat is on and the bowl of Jell-O is cradled in his arms—and he asks her if she wants a bite.

She makes a face.

"They're cute together," he says.

She frowns, walks into the bathroom, brushes her teeth, washes her face. When she comes out, Larry is sitting on the edge of the bed, coat and Jell-O gone.

"Not really," she says. She turns her back to him while putting on the blue flannel pajamas that had been his before she took them for her own.

"Your fly buttoned?" he asks, pointing at the baggy bottoms and probably hinting about her comment earlier that she knew how they could get warm.

Marlene crawls into bed, pulls the covers up to her chin and curls up in a ball. "They'll never last," she says.

Larry stands near the window. "Look at that moon and the clouds." He whistles.

She wants to ask what it was he said to Sylvia. "I don't like the way it sounds," she says.

"Sounds?"

"Russian."

Larry stares out the window, perhaps reconsidering a walk.

Marlene clears her throat, makes a few swishing sounds.

"Oh, no. It's not like that at all. It's beautiful," Larry says.

Marlene resents his saying that it's beautiful, starts to suggest that he might have stayed and talked with Sylvia. She clears her throat, pulls the blankets tighter around her shoulders.

Larry answers by saying something that sounds like "sweet talk." "*Tsveetok*, that's flower." Then he says an entire phrase full of L's and oo's. "That was—"

"OK, OK," she says.

Around the bedroom there are photographs: Larry and Marlene hugging, Larry carrying Marlene in his arms, Larry and Marlene kissing, the honeymoon at Myrtle Beach, Marlene and Larry sitting on a park bench. Lots of history here for just three years. The bedroom is bright with moonlight, and Marlene sees the photographs. She stops short of asking, *What happened?* "I don't think they're going to make it," she says.

Larry opens the bedroom window a crack, undresses, climbs into bed next to her. "Cold," he says.

"I mean they're so different. He doesn't speak her language, and she's always asking him, 'what is the word for . . . .'" Part of Marlene thinks that if Ken and Sylvia do not make it, that the odds somehow increase for her and Larry. Another part of her thinks the opposite.   A gust of wind blows powdery snowflakes into the room, and they sparkle briefly in the moonlight before they fall into the shadows and disappear.

Larry does not disagree, and she assumes that he is thinking too, seeing how difficult and tiring it must be for Ken and Sylvia to talk.

Larry's hand plays with the waistband of her pajamas and then slides up her stomach until his fingertips are brushing the flannel over her breast. "Mmmm," he says.

Marlene knows that in a second he will try to slide the pajama bottoms down or unbutton the fly, but she can't let go, not yet. She has a thought, of all things, about the snow and how the Eskimos have—what?—a hundred words for it. A word for every kind of flake, their texture, the speed with which they fall, how abundantly they fill the sky, their slipperiness. She's on the verge of an important insight, and, if she can concentrate for a minute, it will all become clear to her.

Larry's thumb slides inside the waistband, gently tugs, then goes to the fly and begins to work the button.

Marlene catches his wrist. Now she's thinking of the slipperiness, the elusiveness of emotions. Love, jealousy, fear, loneliness. She understands that Sylvia and Ken might make it after all, that none of us speak the same language. Not really. For a second she can feel Sylvia's loneliness. Marlene thinks if she can only find the right words, explain this to Larry, everything will be okay.

The room grows darker as clouds pass in front of the moon.

"Larry?" she says, stopping his hand before it goes to the next button and thinking of how she will begin.

Larry groans. "What now?" he asks.

Marlene wants to explain, but then Larry's hand, the bright patch of moonlight on the wall, and the words are gone.

Numbers

Lou, our principal, told Liz, his assistant, who let it slip to my friend Janet when they were out drinking that I was "playing with fire" seeing a young boy, a boy Jake's age, and, although he might be over eighteen, it was immortal (he meant immoral)—a woman my age dating someone his.

Lena Berkholtz, who teaches ninth grade history and was once caught *doing it* (not history) with Lou—he was not our principal then; he taught government—on the eighteenth green of the Madison Country Club back in her wild and crazy years before she was born-again, born a second time so to speak, told Jerry that she was not comfortable coming to his back-to-school-party if I was invited because of the rumors she'd heard about me sleeping with "the boy." So Jerry—I've known him for fifteen years—did not invite me. It hurt, yes, but I pretended it didn't and, in fact, picked up a poppy seed bagel from Bruegger's for Jerry on my way to school just to let him know there were no hard feelings, although, to a degree, there were.

Three firsts:
His birthday is December 1st. Twelve-slash-one. For three months we will be twenty and forty-eight, although we are now nineteen and forty-seven, which was the year my parents married.

We first knew there was something between us the day of the earthquake (4.8 on the Richter scale) and, yes, they do occur in northern Ohio (the ground bouncing back up after hundreds of thousands of years beneath the ice-age glaciers). The two of us stood in the doorway of my room, looking at each other wide-eyed and grinning while the building shook and Lou ran up and down the hall telling everyone to stay in their rooms. The ground shaking when you fall in love sounds like a movie cliché but this time it happened.

Summer, Jake is home and we go down to the Grand River. We're eating pizza, talking school, talking fishing, just easy talking, but I worry someone might see us and think something is going on, and to an extent there is. So I say that it might not be a good idea, us being seen together because people talk and we would be one thing they like talking about. I tell Jake about my not being invited to the party and who knows what might be said about him next.

Jake says he's sorry anyone thinks our personal lives are any of their fucking business and would I like the last piece of pizza. That was the first time I ever heard him use the F-word, although I have used it more than once myself. I said, we'll split it.

Two two's and two too's:
I've been divorced two times and have two sons. The youngest will graduate from Ohio State next May. It's been eight years since the last divorce. I swore I'd never get married, never get involved with someone again. Too much pain, too much.

Jake is five foot ten, and has a 3.9 GPA at Indiana University. His favorite radio station is 105.7 Magic. Oldies but goodies. He knows the words to all the songs. Three Dog Night is his favorite. Sometimes, on the way to the river, he rolls down the car window, sticks out his elbow and sings "Never Been to Spain."

My favorite is the contemporary station, 106.5. I like the 4 Non Blondes but do not, can not, sing their songs.

When Jake started kindergarten I had been teaching high school French for ten years.

Numbers that may or may not be important:
I'm not as old as some people think. That was a mistake in the *News Herald* last year when they printed my age as forty-nine after I'd placed thirty-second in a five mile race.

My bathroom scale reads one hundred and twenty when I come back from my morning run but is five pounds light, which usually makes the few who use my bathroom happy.

When Jake went off to college we wrote each other once a month, after Christmas we wrote more. I keep his letters in a size-seven shoe box beneath my bed.

Jake's father got eighteen months for selling pot and Jake didn't talk to him for two years but now his father has reformed and they are closer than they ever were before. Happy ending.

Jake weighs one hundred and sixty. He's thin but strong. He picks me up, hugs me, my feet not touching the floor for close to a minute. Both of us being five-ten, the hugs are eye to eye, hip to hip.

The month after I first slept with Jake I gained six pounds. I took the home pregnancy test twice and both times got one line. Huge relief. Still, I was pretty upset about the six pounds, although many would have said I deserved more.

Lena, who worried I might contaminate Jerry's back to school party, says that I'm having a mid-life crisis. I don't feel crisis-like although if I live to be ninety-six, forty-eight would be mid-life.

Jake asks me to go to the movies, and I remind him of how old I am. "I'm almost forty-eight," I say.

"I'm almost twenty," he answers.

We stop at his house so he can get two movie coupons he left on his dresser. "Want to come in?" he asks.

I shake my head, hunker down in the seat. I can see his stepfather, who shares the same first name as Jake's father, moving inside the house, a man over six foot and weighing two hundred and fifty pounds. Big bones, big muscles, little fat. Maybe he'll walk to the car, say nasty things to me while Jake grabs the coupons. Maybe Jake's stepfather and a couple of uncles will take me for a ride and threaten me to never come around again. But nothing happens, which is good for me but bad for this story because a dangerous ride, a few punches, a gun in the ribs, would spice things up a bit.

"Did your parents say anything?" I ask when we pull into the parking lot at the theater.

"Not a single word," he says.

The movie is *Contact*. We sit in the dark and hold hands, eight tangled fingers, two tangled thumbs.

Jake's mom asked Jake if things were getting serious, then told him to remember that when he was twenty-nine I'd be fifty-seven.

Jake said *serious* was for sickness, crime and global warming. "Things are good," he said.

Once or twice a week, we go down to the Grand River. Jake loves to fish. Bass, bluegill, sometimes trout. But mostly we talk.

Hot evenings we kick off our shoes, jump in.

We float on our backs and let the current carry us a hundred yards downstream before we get out, walk back to the bridge, water dripping from our shorts and T-shirts, and do the whole thing over again. Jake tells me that water is often a symbol for sex in literature. I didn't know water that way but am happy to learn.

Jake leaves his rod and reel at my house. Books too. A dozen. He's always reading. Ray Carver, Carol Shields, Gary Guinn, Gwen Hart. "They rock," he says. When we're at the river, he'll tell me things he's read, and his way of telling makes it seem true, like it really happened and is not just a made-up story.

Jake says, "Tell me about the sixties."

I tell him I was a kid and didn't do drugs or sex or protests but I knew three or four who did.

Jake's laughter bounces across the river and echoes off the bottom of the Vrooman Road bridge.

End of summer comes hard and fast. Jake going back to school, three hundred and thirty miles from where we live here in Fairport, twenty miles from Cleveland. Six hours one way, but Jake says I can make it in five and a half if I avoid the red lights. We circle dates on the calendar: the tenth and eleventh of October.

When I saw the movie *2001: A Space Odyssey* back when I was a teenager, a little younger than Jake, I didn't think it would ever happen. I didn't think 2001 would ever get here. But it's here; it happened. Poof. Just like that.

I count the days until I can see him, although it isn't smart to wish time away. My time, his. I worry that my going, my being around the entire weekend might mess up his study plans, his 3.9, or that his roommates might joke about the old lady.

Being alone, being away from Jake, my mind takes time to catch a breath and worry about other things too. I worry about time going poof. When I'm sixty-five, he'll be thirty-seven. When I'm seventy-nine, he'll be fifty-four.

Alone at night, I do the math of it, subtracting, adding, calculating, trying to make the numbers closer.

Lena says that a relationship like mine and Jake's has one chance in a million, less.

Once a week, on Friday nights, Jake and I talk on the phone until after midnight. It's something we do. It makes me forget the poofing of time. I stretch out on the sofa, bury my toes beneath a blanket and eat brownies while he tells me stories about school or books he's read. It's like floating down the river without the water. Me and Jake, shooting the breeze.

Lena asks if I've had second thoughts, says I'm going to get hurt, that I'll pay a high price for what I'm doing.

At CVS, antiwrinkle cream, the good stuff, runs $11.95 an ounce.

A thirty-five minute phone call to Indiana costs three dollars and fifty cents. (Jake says he has two tickets for the football game and if it doesn't rain, we'll go for a walk around campus.)

Lena teaches history; I teach French, don't understand higher math.

I make reservations for two at the Holiday Inn, there in Bloomington. Seventy-eight dollars a night.

Jake picks up on my fears during the phone calls, figures them out from the length of a pause or the sound of my voice. Jake says, "Don't worry, love is long."

I say, "Yes, yes," don't mention time is fast.

Zeke

Fire

When Zeke returned to Ohio and took the ninth grade science position in our building, we were all happy to have him as a member of our faculty. The veteran teachers appreciated his energy and enthusiasm, and the younger ones admired his outrageous sense of humor. Those who had been in the armed forces—there were four—respected him for his military service, and those who had never served felt they owed him something. Martha Nelson and Sally Baxter, two single teachers, enjoyed his teasing and went out of their way to sit at his table during lunch, frequently sliding chocolate chip cookies or slices of homemade cake onto his cafeteria tray. And even Cheryl Metcalf and Dennis Moore, the two most melancholy, unsmiling teachers in our building, laughed at his ears.

They were as large as two T-bone steaks and nearly covered the sides of his face, but, otherwise, they looked and felt much like human ears. He began wearing them so the students would stop pestering him, interrupting him in the middle of class to ask, "Mr. Earley, did you get a haircut?" When he wore them, he looked like something out of the circus or a Disney cartoon. Later, students standing at their lockers or waiting in the lunch line would say, "Mr. **EAR**ly," and laugh.

Our principal, Mr. Greene, did not seem to mind the ears but he objected to almost everything else. He knew Zeke's students loved him, and, like the rest of us, felt he owed Zeke something.

Zeke often wore the ears to Brewz down on the harbor, where some of us went on Fridays after work to unwind and complain. If Zeke got there before Cooney and Sally, his first-year teaching friends, he'd sit on the wooden bench out front, his bright Hawaiian shirt flapping in the breeze while he watched weekend sailors out of Cleveland dock their boats. Zeke always waved at the people on deck, who waved back and then laughed at his ears.

And drink! Five, six beers were nothing. A skinny guy with hollow legs. We wanted to sit at his table—this was years before the thing with the young girl, before any of us worried about how it might look if we were seen with him. No one minded that he was a rookie; his stories and silliness made us forget the whining and complaining students and their unreasonable parents.

Zeke had only been teaching a month when Joyce, our secretary, discovered her Youngstown State penguin doll missing from her desk. That afternoon she received a ransom note and a picture of the doll sitting on a block of ice. The note demanded a box of Krispee Kreme Doughnuts (powdered) be left on the table in the custodian's closet but warned her that if she told the police, the penguin would bake in the sun.

The following day the doll dangled from a rope outside Joyce's office window and was quickly yanked up and out of sight when she tried to grab it. During lunch the Coca-Cola delivery man waved the doll at her as he pulled out of the drive in his truck. After a few days Joyce gave in to the doughnut demands and left a box in the cus-todian's closet. By noon, the penguin was sitting on her desk, and Zeke's blue shirt was streaked with powdered sugar.

No one knew what would happen next, but Zeke always had something planned.

One night he painted our names on the curb in the parking lot and caused a massive traffic jam the following morning as everyone tried to find their assigned spot. Zeke denied having anything to do with it, but there were specks of yellow paint on his hands, and when told he had spelled Mr. Greene's name without the final "e," he laughed and said, "I know."

Another time Zeke sprayed John Walker in the crotch of his pants with a squirt gun ten minutes before homeroom started, forcing John to sit behind his desk until the spot dried. A few thought he had gone too far even if it was funny. But everyone had grown tired of John's constant insistence we buy the chocolate candy bars his son was selling for summer band camp, and, besides, it was like Zeke had too much energy and couldn't control himself.

For four or five years it went on like this, Zeke entertaining us with his antics or instigating silliness when we least suspected it. He was the best thing that had ever happened at Unity Middle School.

Then the girl came along.

She never rode the school bus but would walk alone the two

miles from her house out on Tyler Lane, walk in all kinds of weather carrying her bright green nylon shoulder bag, maybe the only kid in school not to use a backpack. The bounce in her walk! Those long legs! The full lips and wide smile, that sensuous mouth. But when you saw the animal charms dangling from the shoulder bag or heard her giggle, there was no mistaking she was just a kid.

It wasn't unusual for eighth and ninth grade girls to linger at the desk of a male teacher after class to share a cupcake made in home-economics or to flirt. So no one thought too much of it when she began stopping by Zeke's room after school, but a few of the men wondered what such a pretty girl saw in a goofy guy like Zeke.

Zeke and the girl would sit on the lab tables over in the corner of the room away from the door, and she'd swing those long legs back and forth, back and forth, the hem of her short skirt pulled high above her knees. She never seemed to run out of things to say with Zeke although she hardly spoke to the rest of us. When we passed his room early in the morning or after school, we could hear her talking, words spilling out, all breath and emotion.

And then the girl stayed later and later in Zeke's room, some-times an hour or more after the buses had gone. Her name was Wendy, but no one called her by her name when talking about her and Zeke, it would have seemed like we were making them a couple. Most afternoons, around four, the two of them would walk across the school parking lot and get into Zeke's car. There was talk that he was driving her home, but no one knew for sure where they were going.

In April they showed up at a ninth-grade track meet. Only a few parents and teachers were there, so the stands were mostly empty except for Zeke and the girl sitting in the bleachers, up on the top row, huddled together against the cool, windy day, eating hot dogs, sharing a Coke and laughing. We were horrified by his rela-tionship with the girl, that it could be happening in our building, but we enjoyed it, too, the excitement and drama it brought into our lives, and we would meet in each other's rooms after school to share the latest rumors and speculations.

Zeke stopped coming to Brewz, and we resented that he chose to be with her instead of us. We were annoyed that he didn't realize the trouble he was in.

At first, Mr. Greene pretended not to notice the two of them, pretended not to notice in the way he had ignored the ears, but after a call from Mrs. Young, the president of the PTA, and after some students began talking openly about Wendy and Mr. Early getting married, he called Cooney and Sally into his office, closed the door and suggested they have a talk with Zeke.

"We don't know that there is really anything going on," he said. "Could be nothing. He's young, maybe just poor judgement, but it doesn't look good." He thought it would be better if they said something to him, they were his friends. "He's playing with fire," he added.

Next morning, Cooney went to Zeke's room, before the girl got there. He didn't know how to start so he blurted it right out, "People are beginning to talk, Z."

Zeke watched the door as if he were afraid the girl might walk in and hear.

"It doesn't look good, I mean it looks bad," Cooney said. Cooney wanted to make a joke, something to break the tension, but he couldn't think of anything funny to say and it annoyed him that he had been asked to confront his friend.

Zeke turned away and began writing on the blackboard. "Anything else?" he asked.

Sally talked with him later that day and explained how impressionable young girls are and how they like to pretend they're women. "But they aren't," she said.

Zeke didn't listen to her either and it pissed everyone off. Cooney and Sally were trying to save his ass.

"Do you think he's putting it to her?" Cooney asked that afternoon in the art room when the levy committee met to write postcards requesting parents' support.

"Cooney!" Sally shouted. "They're just down the hall."

Cooney covered his mouth, but it didn't hide the grin.

John Walker shook his head, "Hope not for his sake."

"Her sake," Sally said.

There were rumors that her parents knew and rumors they didn't. Some said her mother liked Zeke; others said she'd never met him. Things we did know: Wendy was an only child; her father was a dentist. Her mother taught dance at the school of Fine Arts and raised Chesapeake Bay Retrievers.

Every bit of information was like a piece of a jigsaw puzzle that we would twist and turn, but the pieces never fit.

We figured it was only a matter of time before Zeke was thrown in jail or fired. We talked about it over our charcoal grills and picnic tables, at Little League games and when we were golfing. The relationship puzzled the women. They studied the girl whenever they saw her, looked at her long legs and compared them to their own. They noticed her small breasts and hips and imagined the lip gloss she wore was bubble gum flavored. How could any man possibly be interested in that? But it scared them, too, and when Zeke and the girl were discussed, wives looked at their husbands as if they were strangers. The men, in turn, felt angry and betrayed, but the more they protested and claimed their own innocence, the more guilty they looked because they had also watched the girl, watched the way she walked and the way her skirt slid up high on her thighs, and they had wondered.

The following year Wendy entered the tenth grade and went across town to the high school. We saw her occasionally, when we ran into her and Zeke at Dairy Queen or the Bad Wolf Barbecue or Vick's Pizza, the girl picking fries or pizza off his plate, maybe taking a lick from his ice cream cone as they leaned towards each other and whispered, their knees bumping beneath the table.

She went out for the track team and Zeke went to her meets, sat in the bleachers down close to the finish line. Before her races she would come over and grab the railing, lift herself up until they were eye to eye. She'd whisper and he'd nod, and then she'd run back to the start while he stood there holding her sweatshirt, watching her take her position in the blocks.

And then the gun would go off and above all the screams and cheers, he'd yell, "W E N D Y !" as she flew around the track, floating on her long, lambent strides. After she won her race, which she always did, she'd turn and give him a little wave, a flutter of her fingers. And Zeke would be on his feet the whole time, grinning, his arms waving in secret semaphore, unconcerned that we were watching.

Most of us were relieved when she graduated and went south to Roanoke College in Virginia on a track scholarship. We were sure the affair would end, but more than a few feared that he might have developed a fondness for young girls, and they worried about whom he might prey on next. But every other Friday, Zeke was the first one out of school, even beating the kids across the parking lot, shirts hanging in the back of his car and a cooler resting on the passenger seat. "Eight hours," he called to Cooney one day as he ran out of his room. He became obsessed with the Weather Channel's Weekend Forecast and complained that the mountains of West Virginia slowed him down.

For two years it went on like this, Zeke racing back and forth, putting thousands of miles on his car, circling the dates on his room calendar when he would see her again. He began a physical fitness program, running the back roads around town and lifting weights with the football players in the gym. He stopped drinking beer, and Sally swore his back porch was stacked floor to ceiling with cases of Coke.

"He's burning the candle at both ends," Harley said one day at lunch. Harley was president of the UTEA and was sure Zeke couldn't continue like this much longer. "It'll be over soon," he assured us. Many eagerly anticipated the day Zeke would pay for his foolishness, but when Zeke's classes scored high on the proficiency tests, Mr. Greene and the parents forgot about him and the girl. They talked about what a good teacher he was and how the students liked him.

Then the trips abruptly stopped. Some guessed her parents had finally warned him off or that she had found someone her own age, and a few assumed the relationship had simply run its wicked course.

Zeke was moody. He ate lunch by himself and stayed in his room after school working on papers or staring out his window. He kept her picture on his desk, the one with her arms stretched high above her head as she crossed the finish line, but he never came down to the lounge and explained what had happened.

His mourning the end of their relationship angered us. We wanted to shake him and remind him that she was a student and what he had been doing was wrong, that he should be thankful the sordid affair ended without lawsuits or the loss of his job. We wanted to tell him that his behavior had been a burden for all of us. A few of the men suspected that he just missed the sex.

Wendy didn't come home that summer, and after awhile Zeke began showing up at Brewz.

Then Zeke met Lisa.

He'd been in Brewz with a psychedelic yellow skateboard

clutched beneath his arm. "My ride home," he said. Some of the men teased him about it, warned him about skating under the influence, and it felt good, almost like old times. Zeke laughed, said, "If those little farts can do it, so can I."

Lisa was an emergency room nurse who worked the night shift at Salem Hospital where she helped treat him. They began dating that week, and within a month were living together.

A couple of days after she moved in, Zeke saw a grocery cart abandoned at the top of Market Street and asked Lisa to ride it down the hill with him. His ankle had healed and the scrapes on his arms and hands had scabbed over. She refused, so he gave it a push and went down by himself. "Zeke! No!" she had yelled.

But Zeke did, and she walked the rest of the way home without him. It was a sore spot between them for several weeks.

Another sore spot was Zeke's drinking. Lisa insisted he stop.

Most of us liked Lisa although there was an edge to her, a bossiness. She had known Zeke for only a few months and was already trying to change him. Nevertheless, Lisa's serious-mindedness and Zeke's silliness balanced each other. She seemed solid, anchored in reality, whereas Wendy—we really tried to avoid comparing them but it was unavoidable—was so airy and light she appeared to float when she walked or ran.

Then, boom, just like that, Lisa and Zeke got engaged and his house got egged. It was the Fourth of July, late in the evening, and when the first egg popped on the side of the house, Lisa thought it was a firecracker. She was about to go power walking and had just finished tying her shoes.

Three more eggs smacked the side of the house. This time Lisa recognized them for what they were. She didn't like some of Zeke's students, didn't like the way they stared at the two of them when they were out eating or picking things up at the drugstore, and she suspected that this was the work of the Doyle twins or Jason White, names she'd heard but faces she'd never seen. She threw the door open and hit the front yard running before Zeke had a chance to stop her.

The egger was thin and Lisa wanted to tackle, wrestle the kid to the ground, inflict a little pain for what had been done. The vandal, wearing a baseball cap pulled down so far it was impossible to see his face, stood beneath the streetlight, watching, waiting.

"I'm going to get you, you son of a bitch," Lisa yelled. We

marveled at her bravery and asked if she didn't know that the kid could have had a knife or maybe even a gun. But we loved this part too, and would have her repeat it over and over while we pictured her racing down the street after some troublemaker, and each time we'd hope that she might catch the egger, knock him to the pavement and then reveal his name.

But in every version of her story the egg thrower stood beneath the street lamp, defiant, not moving as Lisa got closer and closer. Maybe the egger was weighing the odds, maybe considering a fight, then, at the last second, the kid took off. "Took off fast," Lisa would say. "Took off like a ghost, ran down the street faster than anyone I've ever seen."

Zeke fidgeted during her telling of the story. He didn't like the way we looked at him, and when Lisa was finished, he'd quickly change the subject.

Then the engagement was off. Rumors flew as fast as those Fourth of July eggs. Harley said he'd seen Zeke's Toyota down by the Grand River, supposedly a place Zeke and Wendy had frequently gone. "Two people inside," he said. He couldn't see who they were and a few questioned if it had really been Zeke's car. Others heard Lisa had cold feet out of her concern about Zeke's drinking, but there were some who insisted Zeke had never gotten over the girl.

Whatever their problems, Zeke and Lisa got married the following summer. On their honeymoon, a Caribbean cruise, Zeke read a novel, his first since college, and got drunk on rum. That's what he and Lisa talked about when they returned, the book and the sweet rum drinks. Lisa told Miss K. that she worried about Zeke's drinking, but figured it was their honeymoon, and besides, she'd been drinking too. She knew it would be different when they got back to Ohio.

When school started, Zeke was full of his old silliness. He slurped Jell-O from his cafeteria plate and tossed Virginia Cole's rock-hard brownies across the room into the wastebasket. He pretended the sofa in the teacher's lounge was a bobsled and he was in the Olympics, running in place, holding the armrests until Cooney yelled, "Now!" Then he leaped in the air and came down on the sofa with a crash, snapping off the legs and sending all of us to our next class laughing. He lost a bet with his students and paid up by doing the hula at a school assembly; he dropped dry ice in the men's john and, after fog filled the room, walked out claiming he had gas. At Brewz and at the faculty parties, Zeke drank beer with whiskey chasers, drank them fast, like a man gulping water after a marathon, maybe trying to make up for those years when he'd only been drinking Cokes.

Wendy graduated from Roanoke College and moved back to Unity, then went for her master's in teaching at Lake Erie College. She asked Zeke if she could student teach with him, and he, of course, said yes.

Lisa was furious.

Zeke and Wendy—we could no longer call her "the girl"—drank coffee in his room before school and sat on the desks giggling at the end of the day. Only Bill Martin and Heather Krause, two rookie teachers who didn't know the history of the situation, went over and talked with them, welcomed her to our building.

Later, on our way home or out to eat or driving kids to Little League practice, we'd see their cars still there in the lot, as late as five or six o'clock. When Lisa learned about Zeke's late evenings with Wendy, she threatened to kick him out of the house if it didn't stop, but by then the school year was over. The students had a going away party for Wendy, and Mr. Capps, our new principal said she was the best student teacher he'd ever seen.

We marveled at Zeke's luck, that his wife would stay with him and he could have survived all that craziness. Some resented, too, that he'd had a student teacher, a pretty one, and she'd done so well.

Zeke and Lisa had a boy, two years later a girl. At lunch Zeke said he had wanted to name the girl Wendy, but Lisa had said no way in hell. We laughed but weren't sure if he'd been joking.

For the next five or six years, Zeke spent most weekends at Brewz and frequently showed up at faculty parties and picnics smelling of beer. He could no longer hold his alcohol and a few drinks would leave him blurry-eyed and melancholy.

Then, for no apparent reason, Zeke stopped. His hands shook for awhile and he appeared confused, almost afraid. He acted different, as if he was trying to find his rightful place. He was a father, a husband. He had kids in school, a wife, a big house. He was in his forties and was losing his hair. Zeke wasn't sure where he fit in at school, either. Most of our lives had been moving forward while he had been flirting with disaster, and he had trouble falling in step with us, filling in the gaps. There were new teachers and custodians, new friendships and grudges.

He began playing soccer with Andrew and Debbie in his backyard. He went to church and, for two years, was Sunday School Superintendent. He was responsible for our building's United Way Fund Drive the year we set a record; he chaperoned the eighth grade class trip to Columbus, and his bus won the award for best behaved.

When Brewz went out of business, there were jokes it was Zeke's fault.

And then he was at The Anchor, a new sports bar, drinking more than any of us had ever seen him drink, calling the waitresses "Honey" and letting his hand rest lightly on their backs while he tried to say something funny. We didn't crowd around him the way we once had. He sometimes cried after a few drinks and frequently lost his train of thought. He told Cooney: "Wendy said I had to stop."

"Lisa," Cooney said, "you mean Lisa."

There were rumors of Lisa threatening to leave him, and rumors that Zeke was drinking cough syrup and that he kept vodka in his desk drawer. The spider veins in his face grew angry and red, and his eyes had the glazed look of someone in constant pain. His health went downhill faster than the grocery cart he rode down Market Street. That fall he was too ill to teach.

He got better, then he got worse; he was in and out of the Cleveland Clinic.

Then, on Valentine's Day, he died.

Moody's Funeral Home parking lot was full and cars lined both sides of the street. Some teachers and students waited outside in a cool drizzle for nearly an hour before the line moved forward enough for them to step inside.

There were flowers everywhere. Roses and irises and mums and black-eyed Susans. It made us feel good to see that he was remembered like this, but we were frightened, too. Forty-five was too young.

While the line moved forward, we told stories about Zeke, about the time he got in trouble for marching his class to the Dairy Queen during a fire drill and the time he had laughed so hard at a faculty meeting that he had tried to hide under a desk.

Wendy came. She wore a short black dress—more appropriate for a party than a funeral—with a red rosebud pinned over her breast. Her hair was cut short, and a few teachers did not recognize her at first, but there was still that bounce in her step and those long legs. Although rumor said she had married and was teaching in Erie, Pennsylvania, she came alone, and no one could remember getting a good glance at her hand.

Coach Anderson wanted to ask her if she still ran, but he didn't. She walked to the front of the line without saying a word to anyone and stood next to the casket, wadded tissues clenched in her fist. She looked down at Zeke and remembered who knew what, then unpinned the rose from her dress and slipped it in the casket.

We were horrified and glanced at Lisa, who was flanked by her two kids at the other end of the room. If she'd seen or recognized Wendy or what she'd done, Lisa showed no sign of it.

Wendy bent over close to Zeke's face. She whispered, then, without saying a word to any of us, she left.

We were outraged by her audacity and pushed our way forward to see what she had done. When our turn came to view Zeke and say our good-byes, we were surprised at how small he looked and the sallow cast of his skin. But what shocked us most was the rose between his smirking lips. None of us had ever seen anything like it, and we were sure it was one last thing Zeke and the girl had conspired to do. We wanted to tell him to stop grinning and remind him that he had done this to himself. It was as if he and the girl were taunting us, and, as we stood there paying our last respects, we quietly urged each other to remove the rose from his mouth and toss it aside.

But no one could.

Cecil's Highway

Start here, with the story I never told my parents, the other teachers, my wife or kids. It happened in 1972 when I was in my early twenties, but the story could have happened at another time to another person. It continues to replay itself in my dreams and nightmares and is still painful to tell, so let's say it happened to you, let's say it's happening right now.

You're in Maine, alone in the middle of the woods, standing next to your campfire, staring at the little flames licking a wet log. The smoke is stinging your eyes, a light mist is falling and horrible nightmares are playing over and over in your head. You see faces and hear voices and they won't stop looking at you or talking or crying. You're trying to sort them out, the remembered from the imagined, when the man shows up, just slips out of the woods and says, "Howdy neighbor."

You're nervous and jumpy as hell and there's this man, a ghost or hallucination maybe, popping up out of nowhere, bug-eyed in his water-covered glasses. A moan or grunt comes from your throat, the moan scaring you almost as much as it scares the man, and you jump, your body ready to fight or run although you're not built like a fighter. But the man is old and short, not much more than five foot, wears a Boston Red Sox baseball cap cocked at an odd angle, so you hold your ground.

The old-man-ghost-hallucination looks frightened too. His chest rises and falls as he tries to catch his breath. "Sorry," he says. Then he cautiously steps forward, a pot full of raspberries in one hand. "Saw your fire and brought you a present."

You glance around the woods to see if there are others. You don't know how anyone can see your fire—it's small, the smoke sliding sideways off into the woods, and there isn't anyone around for miles. Then you see the Forest Service patch on the pocket of his shirt and remember passing a fire tower on the way in. You look closer, accept that he is alone and harmless, and say, "No thanks," to the berries. It's the first time you've spoken in a week and your tongue doesn't work the way it should, the words come out tangled. You don't want company or small talk, but you don't want to be rude either. *It's not the way you were raised.* "No thanks," you repeat.

The old man pushes the bucket closer, tempting you with the sweet red berries.

You step away from the campfire but the smoke follows you.

The old man rocks back and forth on his heels, wipes his glasses, then smiles as if he is enormously pleased with the way the camp has been set up, the rocks around the fire pit, the clothesline between two white birches. "I'm Cecil," he says. He holds the berries out and nods for you to take them.

He no longer seems afraid of you, which could be good, could be bad. You swallow, make sure your throat and tongue will work this time. You say your name, you almost say *Corporal*, habit being so strong. You take the berries.

Cecil says, "Good, good," studies the trees for a second, then looks at the coffee pot heating above those weak flames.

You can't handle another question, another decision, another distraction. You came here to be alone and, Jesus, here's someone you don't even know waiting for coffee. But you did accept the berries.

"I'd offer you some, but I've only got one cup," you say, and for a second you wonder what you'd do if that one cup cracked.

"Got me own," Cecil answers, pulling a chipped mug out of his backpack. He rolls a rock over to the stove with the toe of his boot and sits, the mug held out, waiting.

He talks about his summers in the fire tower at the top of the hill and his evenings fishing or tramping through the woods. He's retired from the tannery in Hartland, has had three wives, now has "sugar problems" and is supposed to watch what he eats. He looks at you, waits for you to talk, but you don't.

"I was in the Seabees," he says. "Now I'm building my own highway."

". . . building my own highway" doesn't make sense, but you don't ask.

The old man empties his cup but shows no signs of leaving.

"Going to build a cabin?" he asks.

You stand up, toss the rest of your coffee into the weeds. "I don't know," you say. You clear your throat. "You'll have to excuse me."

The old man nods as if he understands. "Come up to the fire tower and visit," he says, then he turns and walks away, disappears into the woods.

Or start here: You've been home less than a month when you read the ad in the *Cleveland Plain Dealer*: *Wooded, secluded land*. And that night you jump in your truck with some clothes and money and a big thermos of coffee and drive sixteen hours straight, from northern Ohio to the middle of Maine, to find it. Seventy-six acres on the side of Chase Hill, miles from telephone and electric lines, televisions, and neighbors, all for forty-eight hundred dollars. You take one look, then drive to the realtor's office in Skowhegan, buy it with the money you squirreled away for the past two years.

You walk over the land, gather dead wood and pine cones for kindling and carry water from a small spring. Beneath a stone fence, you find small, blue bottles with glass stoppers and later set them in a row on a rotting log next to the tent. You find porcupine quills and large black feathers. There are raspberry bushes and deer tracks and signs of bear.

You walk miles every day, refusing to think about anything but the sky or the smell of the pine trees or just getting from one place to another. But then the faces begin crowding in: a toothless old man, a wide-eyed teenage boy, a frightened soldier who looks up a split second before the bullet hits. Sometimes they talk, and, even though you do not know the language, you know what they are saying.

You're drowning in guilt and fear. Shame too. You can't name all the feelings. They don't sort themselves out and you have trouble catching your breath.

Confusion. There's a lot of that. They said that you were the best they'd ever seen, and, in many ways, you were proud. You had been the class clown, not good at anything except making someone laugh and there you were. Even the officers wondered how you did it, and they kept count of your "kills" as if they were points in some game. "Go for a hundred," one urged as the total grew higher and higher.

You reasoned that if you didn't get them, they'd get you or one of your buddies. But you never really believed it. You thought that as soon as you got back to the World it would all be over, but the war came home with you, inside your head. So you hike deeper and deeper into the woods, looking for a place where the voices and faces can't follow.

At the bottom of the hill, you stumble into a cedar bog. It's cool and dark, and the thick canopy of cedar branches and the soft, soggy ground seem to insulate you from the outside world. You sit on a mound of moss and tree roots, feel the moisture seep through the seat of your jeans. You rest your walking stick across your legs. *Perhaps here*, you think.

You take a deep breath, take in the clean smell of cedar, hold it in your lungs, then do it again. Mom and Dad are worried, you can bet on it. They saw your hands shake and worried about the way you were drinking. They looked at each other, then asked if you were okay. You heard them whispering to your sister in the kitchen, telling her to give you space and not ask so many questions. They told you that you could get a job teaching at the junior high or with your dad driving the forklift down in the salt mines. You tried to ignore the questions and suggestions, but then John Bruno from next door stopped over and asked, "How was it over there?" because he was curious and wanted to know.

You told him about the heat and sand and snails bigger than your fist, then you quit talking. That night you left Ohio and headed to Maine.

Your parents have, no doubt, found your note on the refrigerator and wonder if it was something they've said or done. Dad calls your mom everyday from the mine and tells her not to worry, that you'll be fine. But she does worry and he does too, and beneath it all he's more than a little pissed at you for running off the way you did. "Hasn't she worried enough about you?" he'd ask if you were there.

You take another deep breath of that cedar air, hold your hand out in front of you. It's not shaking and you feel better, like this is progress, but then something large, maybe a moose or a bear, crashes through the underbrush, and there's the adrenaline rush, the blood throbbing in your neck, your arms tingling, every muscle ready. You don't move. You wait, sense something behind the trees, watching. You've done this before. Do not, do not, do not, do not move.

You could hold this position for an hour, longer if needed. A minute passes, two. Something dark scurries in the shadows, perhaps the ghosts of men and boys. And you think that they might tear you apart, that someday a hunter will be walking through the bog and find pieces of you scattered about. No one would know what had happened.

You return to the bog every day, hiking deeper and deeper into it, tripping over dead limbs and roots, the ground squishing beneath your feet, water seeping into your boots, until, hungry and exhausted, you stop and rest. Sometimes you sit so quietly you can hear your heart beat as the blood pushes through your ears. Sometimes a twig snaps and it sounds like the safety of a rifle being flipped off and you hug the ground or a shadow, refusing to move until the area is clear.

You have theories. One says get the clean air of the bog inside you, lean back against a tree and let the cedar fragrance disinfect your thoughts. Another theory is to run as far and as fast as you can.

Your father's theory is that if you had played football, maybe gone hunting as a kid, you would have been better prepared. But your dad is wrong. You, who had never shot a rifle in your life, had been the best, could hit a melon or a man's heart at a thousand yards and had done both. You had been so cool and calm about it that they called you "Ice" and even the officers had given you your space, talked about your slow pulse and how you didn't read much and that you didn't smoke as if that helped explain how you could hit targets at distances they thought impossible. It was the one thing you could do better than anyone else, and, when they asked how you did it, you told them about the imaginary string you could feel running from the target to your finger. You just held things steady and pulled.

But they thought you were strange, talking strings, and your drinking made them nervous so they nodded when they saw you and stopped asking.

Sitting in the bog, listening for you're not sure what, you try to empty your mind of obligations and questions about a job, about a girl, about what you have seen and done, but you can't. None of the theories work and you can't take this much longer. Think of the worst nightmare you ever had, the one that made you yell out in your sleep. This nightmare is worse, and you aren't going to wake up and discover it's a dream, not in this world you're not. You're tired of the guilt and fear, the shame, those faces following you. You're attached to that string but this time you're dangling from the other end and it's beginning to pull.

Back at camp you stand beneath the white pine where you hung your duffel bag full of food. The bag hangs from a heavy rope you threw over a tree limb. You pull down on the bag, and the tree limb groans but does not break. You stand there watching the rope swing back and forth, the bag slowly rotate one way then the other.

The next day you walk miles and miles. Your legs are tired, feel like you've been wearing weighted boots, so you try to find a short cut back to camp. If you get tired enough, you'll fall asleep. That's another theory only it hasn't been working. At the top of the hill you hear a voice calling your name.

"Up here."

The steel frame of the tower is completely hidden by the trees and it takes you a few seconds to locate it. You forgot about the old man although you ate the berries.

Up in the sky Cecil leans out one of the open windows and waves you up, then disappears back inside before you can make your excuse, say you have to be going.

On the top step you lean over the side. You are more than a hundred feet above the ground and can feel the tower sway slightly in the breeze. Below, a bird flies from one tree to another.

Cecil opens the trap door. "How's the cabin coming?"

You step up, try to catch your breath, then look at the view, three hundred and sixty degrees of forest and lakes. "I'm thinking," you say.

Cecil raises his eyebrows, leans back on his little stool and offers you a cupcake from his lunchbox.

You shake your head, and he hands you a pair of binoculars, points at a lake in the distance.

You look, don't see anything special, nothing there that the old man might have wanted to show you, but you feel as if you are expected to say something. "Pretty," you say.

"That's where my highway goes," Cecil says, then he pulls out a paper bag and begins to sketch a log cabin, showing you how to put in windows and doors.

It's evening and there are voices off in the distance, but you can't make out what they are saying. Perhaps kids playing on Sibley Pond several miles away. You strain to hear, but the voices fade until there is only the breeze stirring the tops of the trees and the rope creaking as the duffel bag swings back and forth ever so slowly. It's hypnotic.

You are untying the noose around the neck of the bag when Cecil shows up with a school bus seat balanced on his shoulder. "Thought you might be needing some furniture other than rocks," he says. He drops the seat to the ground and collapses on it. He says he went to the town dump in Canaan and found it in a pile of bald tires and broken refrigerators.

"I'd carry it a ways," Cecil explains, "and when I got tired, I'd stop and take a little nap or . . . ." He pulls a paperback book out of his hip pocket and pretends to read.

You and Cecil drink coffee and Cecil talks about the time back in '47 when he and a friend raced motorcycles from Waterville to Bar Harbor. "Mine was an Indian," Cecil says.

You have never heard of an Indian motorcycle.

Cecil says that the headlight on the Indian went out, and he stopped at a hardware and bought a flashlight which he taped to the front of the bike. He talks about the thrill of speeding down back roads late at night with only the dim flashlight and the moon enabling him to see where he was going.

"You win the race?" you ask.

Cecil shakes his head, "No, Jack—that was my friend—took the main roads and got there first," Cecil sips his coffee, then smiles, "but the back roads were more fun." Then he starts another story, this one about getting lost in the woods, but before he finishes, he nods off.

You put sticks on the fire and stare at the flames. Racing a motorcycle down a country road is something you would have enjoyed. You are jealous that the old man can fall asleep so easily but wonder, too, if perhaps something serious is wrong with him, maybe the sugar problem.

For an hour or two your mind is full of crazy thoughts. You wonder if the old man has ever thought about jumping from the top of the fire tower. Then you think about bullets, that one of the bullets you shot has not fallen to the ground, that something is wrong with it or gravity and that it will keep circling the earth, punching holes in people's heads and someday it will find you. You try to pull your thoughts back by thinking about racing on a motorcycle. Your pile of sticks is getting low when the fire pops and sparks float up toward the stars. Cecil's eyes open, "Want to go for a ride?"

You figure the old man is dreaming or has forgotten that it's late or maybe where he is.

He stands up and motions toward the old logging road. "I'll show you," he says.

It's well past midnight when the two of you arrive at his Bronco, which is parked behind the forest service cabin. Even in the dark, you can see the broken antenna, the side mirror hanging by a wire and the cracked windshield.

Despite its appearance, the Bronco starts as soon as he turns the key, but instead of heading for the logging trail or the road that leads to town, Cecil aims straight for the woods.

"Whoa!" You yell, which you will think about later, wonder why you had worried about getting killed when you were planning to do it yourself, and you'll be pleased too, as if this might have marked the beginning of some turning point, that an old man in a beat up truck still had the capacity to startle you. But for now, Cecil ignores the warning and drives between two trees, narrowly missing one.

"The Cecil B. Davenport Highway," he says.

You bounce around rocks, knock limbs and branches aside, run over saplings and barely miss crashing head first into a white pine that is nearly as wide as the truck. Occasionally, Cecil stops, looks, backs up, turns. "Different at night," he says.

Repeatedly, you appear to be lost and suggest that it is time to head back. Each time, Cecil nods, rubs his chin, then lurches forward in a new direction. "A fire road," he calls it, and it has taken him three years to clear. This is his first trip.

Near the bottom of the hill, you approach a fast running stream. You press your hands against the dash and yell, "No!"

The Bronco stops inches short of the steep bank, and Cecil leans over the steering wheel, motions for you to get out and look.

It's a straight drop. "Can't make it," you say, standing in the glare of the headlights and indicating with your hands that it is a good three foot down. You take a deep breath and climb back into the truck.

Cecil grins, hits the gas and the Bronco plunges forward, careens down the embankment, through the stream and squirms up the other side. The headlights point at the top of the trees, and loose tools under the seat slide backward and clang against the tailgate. A few minutes later, Cecil stops the Bronco and motions for you to drive. "I'm tired," he says.

You have no idea where you're going, but you feel a little safer now that you're behind the wheel. You follow the old man's directions as best you can. Sometimes he points and you have to watch his hand at the same time you are trying to avoid a tree. Branches slap the windshield and doors; rocks and logs scrape and screech along the bottom, maybe putting holes in the oil pan or gas tanks. Every time you hesitate, Cecil waves you forward. Eventually, you stop worrying about where you are going or if you are lost or if the gas gauge needle bouncing on empty is accurate. You lean forward, try to follow the trail.

Cecil motions for you to stop and turn off the engine, then fumbles in his backpack behind the seat. You suspect you are lost and that you will have to hike back, that the old Bronco will never make the return trip even if you could find the way, which you know you can not. The truck is stuck here forever. You are tired, numb from all the bouncing. It will take hours for you and the old man to find your way through the woods. You wonder if the old man can do it.

The engine ticks as it cools.

You crank the window down, and a grouse flies out of the brush, startling something loose inside you. Cecil pulls stale cake carefully wrapped in wax paper out of his backpack and offers you a piece. He brushes the cake crumbs off his shirt, pushes his baseball cap back on his head.

The night sky begins to lighten. You think a town or a city is up ahead, then realize it's almost dawn. You have lost all sense of direction and time, can not tell where you are, how far you've come or how far you have to go. But you're hungry. You take the piece of cake, unwrap it. The icing is hard and dry but sweet.

Start here.

Roger Hart has taught high school science in
Painesville, Ohio, and college English at Virginia
Western Community College. He holds a degree
in creative writing from The McGregor School of
Antioch University and was a recipient of an Ohio
Artist's Fellowship. His work has appeared in such
journals as *Ambergris*, *The Ohio Writer*, *Other
Voices*, *Willow Springs*, and *Passages North*. He
and his wife, the poet Gwen Hart, are presently
students in the MFA program at Minnesota State
University.